CHAPTER 1

*K*elly Cole had it all together, or at least that's what she wanted everyone to believe. She'd been dating an artist, a painter by the name of Rio, and her life had been solid.

Emphasis on the words *had been*.

Everything had been in order, as she liked it, until she came home early one day to find Rio in bed with her best friend of six years. Their bodies were entwined in the most intimate of ways, legs dangling off her formerly perfect Pottery Barn bed - which she'd later taken a sledgehammer to just before leaving town.

Now, four weeks later, she was left with the shambles of her former life. At the request of her personal assistant, Kelly had taken a full month off to deal with her anger and sadness over losing a year-long relationship. Four weeks wasn't nearly long enough to leave her bitterness behind.

And she still needed a new bed.

Running her health spa had been the one constant in her life for over two years now, but losing Rio was difficult. No, he really wasn't her type with his free spirit nature and longer-than-she-liked hair, but he was good looking and easy to be with most of the time. She was organized and "tightly wound", as her assistant, Maggie, had often said. But Rio was like a free-flowing river with absolutely no direction.

And now he and her former best friend, Abigail, were "living on love" in Hawaii from what she'd heard. And here she was, in the tiny north Georgia mountain town of Whiskey Ridge, running The Spirit Spa, all alone yet again.

Kelly had carefully constructed her life over the last few years. Her father, in prison for several more years after way too many drug convictions and questionable behavior, was long gone from her life. She'd been raised by addicted parents, and her mother still struggled with a lot of her own demons. Kelly tried to have the relationship with her from time to time, but it never worked out. Having a relationship with someone who obviously has mental issues isn't easy.

For the last four weeks, she'd forced herself out of her cottage home that sat on an acre, and went to

STARTING OVER

RACHEL HANNA

Maggie's aunt's beach house in South Carolina. It gave her some much needed time to decompress and think about her next steps in life.

Yet she still didn't really have an answer.

Sure, she'd love to have a boyfriend, but so far guys hadn't stuck around for her special brand of insanity. Over the years, she had found herself getting more "tightly wound".

Her home had to be super clean.

Her spa had to be perfectly quiet and serene for her patrons. Well, maybe more for herself.

Her yard was always freshly mowed and manicured.

Everything was perfect in Kelly's world, except for her heart. It was, and really always had been, shattered into a million pieces that just couldn't be cleaned up. Her heart was the biggest mess in her life, and she seemed completely incapable of cleaning it up.

"I'm about thirty minutes away," she told Maggie as she drove around the bends of the mountain roads near Whiskey Ridge. The small Georgia town had been a respite from her crazy growing up years in Atlanta, and it was the place she planned to stay until she was old and gray herself.

With its friendly people and quiet atmosphere, Whiskey Ridge was like going back in time. It was the epitome of small-town America with a real drugstore and a barbershop that stayed full all the time. Even though she certainly hadn't grown up in the 50s, Whiskey Ridge reminded her of that era when people moved at a slower pace and everyone knew everyone else.

"How was your trip, boss?" Maggie asked, chomping on her gum, a habit that drove Kelly up the wall but she'd never tell her friend. She didn't want to hurt her feelings, but that constant smacking and spearmint aroma in the air grated on her last nerve sometimes.

"Good. Quiet. Enlightening," Kelly lied. Instead, it had been lonely. Boring. Useless. She was still angry, seething more like it. She'd spent most of the four weeks thinking of ways she could inflict pain on Rio and Abigail from thousands of miles away. Maybe a voodoo doll, she thought, and when she found herself Googling the idea and buying pins at the local drugstore, she decided it was time to come home.

"Glad to hear it. Abigail called you about a week ago," Maggie said quickly, as if she was trying to get the words out as fast as possible so Kelly couldn't shoot the messenger.

"What?" Kelly choked out.

"Wanted to apologize for her 'lapse in judgment', she said. I told her I was fairly certain your response would be to kiss your butt," Maggie said, her sharp wit and uncanny knack of saying whatever she thought coming across the phone line clearly.

Kelly giggled, the first time a laugh had left her lips in weeks. "Thanks, Mags. That is totally what I would've said." Actually, it probably wasn't. Although Kelly had a lot of those kinds of thoughts rolling around in her head, she'd always had a problem confronting people. Wanting to keep the peace, she probably wouldn't have said much of anything and hung up on Abigail. And that's why she was all the more glad that she had a friend like Maggie who would say what she didn't feel like she could say.

"She said Rio feels awful too, and that they wish you a lifetime of happiness. Then she rambled on about their nightly luaus and some kind of weird fruit they eat in Hawaii a lot…"

"Okay, okay. I don't want to hear anymore," Kelly said, already exhausted from her long drive. "I'll stop by there in a few minutes before I head home."

"Not necessary, Kel. I've got things handled here, just like I have for four weeks. Go home. Take a nap. Feed your cat."

"Dang it! I forgot to pick up Tux!" she said, doing a U-turn in the middle of Main Street. Her cat, black with a white chest, had been with her for almost eight years now. He was her most trusted companion and snobbiest friend, but she loved him.

"Relax. I picked him up earlier and took him to your house on my lunch break," Maggie said. Kelly stopped the car in a parking space in front of the local assisted living center and put her head on the steering wheel.

"Thanks," she said softly. "I'll see you tomorrow."

"Good plan," Maggie said before hanging up the phone. Kelly stared at the assisted living center for a moment as the startling and altogether frightening image of herself living there alone without ever having been married or having kids floated through her mind. Maybe her heart just wasn't meant for love. Maybe the only real love she'd ever have would come in the form of a black and white cat who mostly ignored her and occasionally peed on her favorite arm chair.

And so she'd go home to him.

As KELLY DROVE up to her spa the next morning, she felt some normalcy coming back to her life after weeks of turmoil. It had been hard to go home last night without Rio there to greet her with one of his amazing Brazilian dinners. She didn't really miss him as much as she missed his Churrasco and Brigadeiro for dessert.

There were a couple more cars in the parking lot than she would've expected so early on a weekday, but otherwise everything looked like it normally did. Maggie's little beater of a car sat parked under the tall oak tree on the corner of the property, its back passenger window still taped into place as it had been for months now.

She loved her spa. It gave her some semblance of peace, and that had been hard to come by during her adolescent years. Rio had often told her that she wasn't really living her life, but was too busy hanging onto the past by controlling the present. He didn't control anything, including his own income, instead preferring to float through life on love and fun. But how long could that last?

The spa was located in a large, old Victorian house just off the town square in Whiskey Ridge. It was white with hunter green shutters and a large wrap around porch. The cobblestone walkway led straight from the small parking area up to the front steps, and Kelly had added small gardens on both sides of the walkway to give it more curb appeal. She loved seeing her red and pink roses in full bloom.

Although she didn't own the building, her landlord had given her a longterm lease of five years at a great rate, mainly because the upstairs hadn't been rented out in years. Frankly, the landlord seemed to really need the income. Kelly didn't feel bad about her great deal because her business added to the community and changed people's lives, in her unbiased opinion. And one day she hoped to expand upstairs, although she'd looked up there once and got creeped out by the cobwebs and musty smell. There was a spider up there that gave her nightmares for a few days too, so she'd just stay on the main floor for awhile, thank you very much.

Her goal was for spa clients to long for the quiet solitude of The Spirit Spa, and she worked hard to make sure that happened. Set back on a large lot, it was rare to even hear a passing firetruck. Instead, the loudest sounds at The Spirit Spa were the birds chirping and singing in the oak trees surrounding the property.

"Mags?" she called as she walked through the door. Everything looked like it did four weeks ago, with the exception of a new display table set up in the foyer showcasing a line of massage oils and facial masques. Maggie did a very good job at merchandising and maximizing the number of extra sales they made. The spa definitely wasn't a money making powerhouse - yet - but it paid the bills and gave her a purpose.

"Hey, boss!" Maggie said, grinning as she grabbed Kelly in a big hug. It had taken Kelly awhile to get used to Maggie's warm nature when they first met. Maggie was a hugger. She didn't care if she knew you or not; she was going to hug you. The mailman. Clients. Her doctors. It just didn't matter to Maggie Dale. Everyone deserved a hug. Except Rio. She'd hated him, and there were no hugs for him. In fact, she'd said on more than one occasion that she wouldn't spit on him if he was on fire. Not the worst thing to say except she'd said it to his face without shame.

Maggie had fiery red hair, all natural, and the palest skin Kelly had ever seen. She was not a tanning queen herself, but the words "porcelain skin" had Maggie's picture next to them in the dictionary. Her bright blue eyes were big and round, and she had one of the best smiles on the planet.

"Good to have you back," Maggie said, holding Kelly's arm as they walked from the foyer into the office, shutting the door behind them. Clients usually didn't start arriving until after 10 AM, so they still had a good hour to chat and catch up on all the gossip for the past four weeks.

"Good to be back. I love the beach, but I realized I'd never want to live there full time."

"Did you swim a lot?"

"At first, but then I just sat and watched the ocean, shopped, read books. Seethed with primal anger."

Maggie smiled sadly. "I'm sorry, girl. I know losing Rio has been tough… the dirtbag." She always liked to add a little something at the end of comments about Rio. Dirtbag was her favorite, but there were a couple of others that would've been bleeped out on TV.

"You know, it's not losing Rio that was tough as much as feeling betrayed by him and Abigail. I've been betrayed far too much in my life," Kelly said, sighing as she sat down behind her mahogany desk, one of the only splurges she'd made when she started the spa. The antique desk set her back almost a thousand dollars, but she adored it. "And the realization that I'm no closer to settling down and starting a family than I was a year ago."

"Well, today is a new start. You'll find somebody, Kel. Somebody who's worthy of you," Maggie said. She truly was the eternal optimist.

"I don't want another man, Mags. Trust me. I'm done. I'll be celibate for life, and maybe I'll check into becoming a nun."

"No… Their outfits are all wrong," Maggie said shaking her head. "Black is supposed to be slimming, but have you ever seen a slim nun?"

Kelly shook her head and laughed. If there was one thing Maggie could always do, it was make her laugh and forget her problems for a few minutes. Unfortunately, they always came back.

"Listen, I do have a bit of news I need to share," Maggie said, a look of anxiety sweeping across her face as she bit her bottom lip. If Maggie was nervous, something was really wrong because she didn't let things bother her like Kelly did.

"You're not quitting are you?" Kelly asked, putting her forehead on the desk. She just couldn't take another piece of bad news, and losing Maggie would be like losing her right arm. Or a kidney.

"Of course not!" Maggie said. Kelly sat back up

and looked at her friend, thankful that the news couldn't be as bad as she thought.

"Then what?"

"We have a new tenant upstairs. He moved in last week."

"He?"

"Yeah. I haven't seen him yet, but the landlord called and let me know since we'll be sharing parking and the foyer area. And the kitchen, of course."

A feeling of possession welled up inside Kelly's stomach. This was *her* place. That was *her* parking lot. That was *her* foyer. And if he even thought about touching her salad in the refrigerator, they may just come to blows.

"What kind of business is it?" she asked.

"I think some kind of workout place. The landlord was kind of tight lipped about it, really."

"Did you ask any questions, Mags?" Kelly said, pursing her lips. Maggie was notorious for not asking enough questions, which was one reason she'd managed to get herself into trouble dating the wrong types of guys over the years.

"Some..."

"Ugh. I was hoping to get that space for the spa next year."

"Well, maybe he won't be here long."

"Doubtful. Once he sees how great this location is, he'll probably stay forever." Kelly was starting to hate her own pessimistic demeanor lately. Where had her optimism gone?

"She said he will open his doors tonight," Maggie continued.

"Tonight? But, there's no sign out there or anything. How does he plan to get clients?" she asked, standing and pacing behind her desk. She didn't even know this guy yet and already she wanted to poke his eyes out with a fork.

"I don't know, but I'm sure it'll be fine, boss. You're back, and your clients will be so glad to see you. Betty Sue Canton will be in at ten, and then we're booked until three."

The Spirit Spa had a unique schedule. Kelly opened the doors at ten on weekdays, but she closed up at three. Then, she came back from six to nine for her clients who couldn't come during the day. It was a grueling schedule, for sure, but it made her clients happy. And what else did she have to do at night? Yeah, that would be a big, fat nothing.

"And Cat will be here at six?" Kelly asked, referring to her staff yoga teacher who taught night classes.

"Yes. She and Jeremy broke up a couple of weeks ago, so she's been going through her own issues lately."

"Men suck," Kelly said.

"That they do."

"What about you? Any luck on the love front?"

"Nope. I think I'm too much woman for most guys," Maggie surmised. She wasn't overweight, but was curvy. And loud. And opinionated. Most guys around Whiskey Ridge couldn't put up with her for long, and Kelly could see why. She was tons of fun, but a lot of woman for just an average guy. Maggie would require a superhero kind of guy.

Truthfully, Kelly was a little jealous of Maggie in several ways. She had a fun-loving attitude that didn't seem thwarted by any life challenge, although she'd had many in her past. Her hair was memorable, unlike Kelly's dull brown locks that were more wavy than curly and landed just past her shoulders.

Maggie didn't have a boyfriend currently, but Kelly felt she had more options because her larger than life personality drew people in. Men, women, children... even animals. Maggie had an energy about her, and Kelly felt dull. There was just no other word for it. Dull.

"There's a special guy out there for you, Mags. I just know it," Kelly repeated, as she had a million times in the years they'd known each other.

The rest of the day went off without a hitch, just as usual. Kelly made sure that she ran a tight ship. While clients felt comfortable and serene at The Spirit Spa, Kelly was like a frazzled puppeteer in the background, making sure all the parts and pieces of her business were running like clockwork.

By the time three o'clock rolled around, she was

ready to go home for a few hours, feed Tux and put her feet up until she headed back to work at six. They'd seen only five clients all day, but she'd put her heart and soul into each of them. Facial for Betty Sue Canton, massage for Olivia Dane, Reiki energy treatments for two others and nutritional counseling for Ava Enders. All of Whiskey Ridge's elite had been in to see Kelly on her first day back.

At least some people appreciated her.

As she drove down her long driveway at home, she was aching to take a deep breath and drink a nice cup of tea. But when she looked in her rear view mirror as she parked in front of her garage, she caught a glimpse of something.

CHAPTER 2

*N*ot wanting to interrupt a quiet moment, Kelly gingerly got out of her car and closed the door. She crouched behind a big shrub near her front door and watched, as she had done a few times in the past several months when this had happened before.

She remembered it like it was yesterday, and it haunted her even now. First, there was a loud crash, shattering the quiet of Sycamore Street. Then there was smoke, then fire and screams. It was the screaming she could still hear in her nightmares.

Now, all that was left was a memorial cross and some plastic flowers that had been erected at the corner of her property. It had been a whole year now, but the memorial remained. She would never remove it herself, and so she assumed she would have occasional visitors to the spot where they lost their loved one.

When it happened, she'd been home around the same time of day, taking her break from work. The crash had startled her as she took a quick nap before heading back to work. At first, she wasn't sure what it was, but when she looked outside, she only saw a mangled mess of metal wrapped around a large oak tree. Smoke was already billowing from the wreckage. She grabbed her cell phone, quickly dialed 911 and then ran toward the smoke, dropping her cell somewhere along the way.

There was no time to talk. She needed to help this person, and she'd really tried for the few minutes she'd had before the car went up in flames. The ambulance arrived, but it was far too late to do anything, and Kelly sat on the rock wall next to her mailbox, sobbing into her hands out of frustration and despair. She didn't know the woman inside, but she was sure she had family somewhere. People would obviously miss her greatly, and the thought made her heart hurt for those strangers who had no idea that their loved one was gone.

And now, she could see someone visiting the site yet again. Most of the time, she couldn't really tell who it was as it was such a distance. But today, she could see that he wore a baseball cap and seemed to be in his late thirties. He knelt beside the cross, kissed the end of his fingers and touched it. Her heart ached. What a loss he must feel.

Feeling like she was interfering in something sacred, Kelly keyed the lock to her house and went inside, her stomach churning with memories from that day.

* * *

PULLING BACK into The Spirit Spa for her evening routine, Kelly was surprised when she had a hard time finding a parking space. The lot was small anyway, but now it was packed with cars which was highly unusual.

She jumped out and ran inside, the roar of noise apparent. The Spirit Spa was a quiet place of serenity and balance. Tonight, it sounded like the dull roar of a mall was penetrating her cocoon of peace, and she didn't like it. Not one bit.

"Cat, what's going on?" she asked as her yoga teacher met her at the door.

"The new business opened its doors tonight," she said with a sly smile.

"Why are you smiling?" Kelly asked, her eyebrow cocked.

"Well... I'm not too sure you're going to like this..."

"Like what?" Kelly asked, but Cat didn't get a chance to answer before she heard shouts coming from upstairs. "What in the hell…" Kelly said before running up the stairs, taking them two by two, which was quite a feat with heels on.

She swung open the door to the large space that had been created upstairs years ago when the landlord had removed the walls between several of the bedrooms. She was stunned at what she saw. Blue and red mats now covered the hardwood floors, and mirrors lined one wall. Ninja silhouette stickers were on another wall and there were at least ten people dressed in white uniforms moving slowly around the room while shouting words she couldn't understand.

One man was standing at the front of the room wearing a white uniform too, but he had a black belt on. Assuming this was their "leader", Kelly started waving her hand from the doorway to get his attention. He looked at her, obviously irritated that she was interrupting his class, and then returned his gaze to his students.

"Cha Rytt," he said as each student stood at attention and slapped their arms by their sides. "Kyung Yet!" he called, and then they all bowed before he released them. He started writing on some index cards, completely ignoring Kelly who was still standing in the doorway.

"Um, excuse me?" she said, more than a little irritated now. "Hello?" When he didn't look up, she stepped onto the red mat with her stiletto heels and that immediately caught his attention.

"Hey, hey… The mat is for students only, and definitely not for chicks wearing heels," he said, a cocky smile on his ruggedly handsome face. Wait, what? She wasn't thinking clearly, obviously. This guy was a jerk. He called her a chick. And suddenly she had an urge to bite his lower lip.

"Then how about answering me?" she said, stepping back off the mat. He crouched down and rubbed the indentation from his mat before standing up to meet her gaze again. He smelled like a mix of cologne and well-earned sweat, and she wanted to get a closer whiff but thought better of it.

"These floors are expensive. And how do you even stand up in those things?" he asked, referring to her red patent leather heels, which were killing her feet at the moment.

"Really not the point of this conversation," she said through gritted teeth. Who was this guy?

"How can I help you, ma'am?" he asked, bowing. The sarcastic smile on his face made her want to slap him, and then maybe kiss him. And then probably slap him again.

Dang, he was good looking. Jet black hair. Thick. Wavy. Perfect for running her fingers through. Olive skin, dark in comparison to her pale tone. Green eyes that were a color she'd never seen before. A chiseled jawline with just a hint of stubble…

"Ma'am?" he repeated, smiling again at how obvious she was in her staring at him.

Kelly cleared her throat and stood up straighter. "Your business here… is too loud."

"What?"

"I own The Spirit Spa downstairs. I've been here for two years. Our clients prefer a calm and serene environment, Mr.…."

"Maverick."

"Maverick?" she repeated.

"Quinn Maverick," he said, holding out his hand to shake hers. What kind of a name was Quinn Maverick? Sounded like a stage name or a rockstar. Or a cowboy.

She shook it, feeling the warmth of his grip and the size of his massive hand. How tall was this guy? Had to be at least six foot two. Wonder if his abs were rock hard…

"And you are?" he asked.

"Oh. Kelly Cole," she stammered, pulling her hand from his and struggling to regain her composure. "As I was saying, The Spirit Spa prides itself on being a place that our clients can come to get away from the noise of their day and their own stress."

"Nice elevator pitch," he said with a dry chuckle. She ignored the comment and continued.

"So, I would appreciate it if you and your students could keep it down up here. Thanks," she said, turning on her heel and heading for the stairs before she did something stupid.

"Sorry, but no can do, Miss Cole," he said, turning back toward the mat.

"Pardon?" She swung around and almost lost her footing which would have caused a nasty fall down the hardwood stairs. She really shouldn't be wearing stilettos.

"I said I can't do that. This is a karate studio, Miss Cole. We shout and yell and spar and kick and jump. We're not doing tai chi or mime training."

"That's just not going to work for me!" she screeched a little louder than she would've liked. This guy was really getting under her skin.

"Well, there's nothing in our lease prohibiting noise, Miss Cole. The landlord was fully aware of what my business was when we signed, and she was more than happy to have us here." How could someone be so good-looking and yet so irritating at the same time?

"Of course she was. She's been trying to rent this place for months," she muttered under her breath. If she'd only known that the landlord was going to go this route, maybe she would've rented the space herself and just held onto it. Who was she kidding? She never could' Andve afforded that anyway.

"Yes, she was," he said. What, did he have the hearing of a bat? "And, just so you know, if she hadn't rented it to me, she was going to lose this property to the bank which would have landed your peaceful butt on the street."

"Are you always this much of a jerk?" she asked, closing the gap between them and staring into his deep green eyes.

"Maybe. Keep coming up here, and you'll find out soon enough." His jaw was now clenched, and she could see the muscles in his neck tightening as they disappeared behind his collar. She tried desperately not to think about where those neck muscles led.

"Is that a threat, Mr. Maverick?" she asked, suddenly wondering if maybe she shouldn't be challenging a black belt, but feeling a little bit turned on by their exchange. She really needed a date. Soon.

"I don't threaten women, Miss Cole. I'm a black belt in taekwondo and a Southern gentleman, but I don't take kindly to demands that aren't warranted or backed up by my lease. You might have been here first, but I'm here now, and I plan to grow my business. If you have a problem with that, I suggest offering earplugs to your precious, uptight clients. Now, if you'll excuse me," he said as he shut the door to the studio and Kelly was left standing there with her mouth gaping open.

* * *

QUINN MAVERICK WAS a man's man. He had a motorcycle. He drank the occasional beer. He was a black belt in karate. But dang if a beautiful woman couldn't turn him to mush in a heartbeat.

The last woman who'd done that had stolen his heart and then broken it. He wasn't about to open himself up to that kind of torture again. No, a life of meaningless sex or celibacy sounded a hell of a lot better than loving again.

And why was he thinking about love anyway? She was just an uptight sexpot wearing her red stiletto heels and almost ruining his new floor. She was beautiful, with her porcelain skin and long, brown hair, but she was wound tighter than a yo-yo, and he wasn't signing up for a crazy woman right now.

He was building a business. He was a focused entrepreneur. And right now, he was in need of a cold shower.

* * *

"So, did you meet the new guy upstairs?" Cat purred, true to her name. She was waiting at the bottom of the staircase, her long blond hair molded into a perfect bun, and her black yoga pants hugging her even more perfect butt. Ugh.

"I did, and he's the world's biggest jackass," Kelly said as she brushed past Cat and went straight into her office.

"Seriously? He's a fine looking specimen to me!"

Cat said grinning like a... Cheshire cat. How appropriate.

"Well, good looks can only take you so far in life. His attitude is horrendous."

"Kelly, don't take this the wrong way, but you need to lighten up. Have some fun. Live a little." Cat was the ultimate free spirit. Nothing bothered her, and maybe it was all the yoga. She just floated through life with her perfect abs and tight butt, and men followed her around like they were lost. Surely she'd have Mr. Maverick in bed within the week, and that thought made Kelly feel a little... jealous?

"Cat, don't you have a class to teach?"

"Oh, hell, you're right!" Cat jumped off the edge of the desk and ran across the hall.

Kelly stared out across her now full parking lot, and sighed. It was May, and that meant she was about to experience the one day of the year she dreaded most. Mother's Day. Not because her mother was dead. No, her mother was still very much alive... if you could call that "living". But Kelly would have to go visit her in Atlanta, and the thought made her skin crawl.

CHAPTER 3

*K*elly pulled onto her mother's short concrete driveway, and her heart was already starting to pound and skip. It was a quirk of hers. Anytime she got anxious, her heart had its own little parade complete with a drum line and drunk cheerleaders. She struggled to catch her breath, willing herself not to have a full-on panic attack like the last time she visited.

One year ago. Mother's Day again.

She'd promised her mother she would come once a year on that date, but no other visits. She just couldn't take it. No Christmas dinners at mom's house. She was welcome to visit Kelly, but she never did.

Kelly's sister, Vivienne, had long since abandoned their mother, opting instead to marry a surgeon and move to France, the birthplace of her super cool name. She'd been born Vicky, but she'd complained it was a "redneck" name and changed it when she left home. After a brief stint as a stripper and then an escort - not redneck at all apparently - she'd managed to snag a surgeon she'd given a lap dance to and cash in.

But not Kelly. Nope, good old dependable Kelly had stayed close by, sending her mother money when she had it to spare, and visiting her once a year.

To an outsider, her once a year visit from just two hours away was the sign of a very bad daughter. Who leaves their mother for a whole year without coming by and checking on her occasionally? Kelly had a hard time explaining it to people without giving her life story, and that just wasn't going to happen. Her life story was hers, and it was better left unsaid.

She couldn't procrastinate any longer or her mother would come outside in her bathrobe and embarrass her, so she turned off the car and stepped out.

As she stepped out of the car, she felt the dead leaves crunch beneath her feet which was an odd sensation given that it was May in Georgia and those leaves had fallen last winter. But her mother wasn't one for yard work, and the driveway had more leaves than concrete.

Sadly, Kelly had worn her winter boots today in

preparation for seeing her mom. She looked ridiculous, really, wearing a tank top, capri pants and a pair of winter boots. But she knew it was necessary given the state of her mother's home.

She walked to the door and knocked, knowing full well that the bell hadn't worked in years. She'd grown up here, in this house, but it looked like a strange place to her now. It certainly wasn't home, but then again it never was.

She could hear noise inside the house as her mother made her way to the door. Thankfully, she was still in pretty good shape given the rough life she'd led. All the years of drinking and drugs had certainly taken a toll on her health, with one previous cancer battle many years ago, but she seemed to have bounced back as well as could be expected.

Kelly heard the lock being turned as her mother slowly pulled the door open. She couldn't open it all the way, given the amount of trash and junk scattered about the house. It had been a full year since she'd seen her mom, and she kind of dreaded the thought of having to see just how bad the house had gotten in the last twelve months.

She smelled the house before she saw it. It was a hard smell to describe to someone else. Mold mixed with cat urine was the easiest way to begin explaining it, but it had such a bite that her eyes were already stinging.

"Kelly, my baby!" her mother said, as she always did. Today she was wearing gray sweatpants and a ratty T-shirt. She used to send her mother nice clothes, but she never seemed to wear them anyway so Kelly had given up years ago. She imagined they were now buried somewhere deep within the piles of possessions her mother lived amongst.

"Hey, Momma," Kelly said, slowly reaching in to the doorway to give her mother a hug. It was difficult with all the junk keeping them apart, literally and figuratively. But Kelly was well aware that one day her mother would be gone from this earth, and she didn't want to have any guilty feelings about not embracing her when she could.

Her mother smelled of smoke and a mixture of the smell from the house. Kelly's gag reflex started to activate, as it usually did when she visited. She leaned her head back outside and took a deep breath. It would be the last deep breath she took for the next couple of hours.

"Come on in!" her mother said, as if she was about to host an elegant dinner party. She was completely oblivious to the problem, and always had been. She and her sister had grown up in the house, and Vivienne had run away as soon as possible. Of course, she was Vicky back then.

Her mother backed up, and Kelly had to push on the door with her shoulder to even get inside. She was thin, just like her mother's build, but there was barely enough space to slide through. When she finally got her first glimpse of the living room, she wanted to cry. It wasn't like she had a lot of good memories there, but there had to have been at least twice the junk there was twelve months ago.

Her mother had made the mess, that much was certain. But no one should live like that. And there was no reason for it which was the frustrating part. She'd had to come to terms over the years with the fact that her mother had mental issues of her own. She didn't know where they came from, she just knew they existed. The years of drug and alcohol abuse had to have been caused by something, and now the hoarding was her addiction.

"Oh, Momma, how do you live like this?" was all Kelly could manage to say. She wanted a gas mask right now, and she tried to take slow, shallow breaths to keep from inhaling too much of the toxic air. The living room was full of junk. Her mother liked to say that she was a "collector", but there were no collections here. There were just piles of trash, newspapers and magazines and random broken items that her mother had been climbing over for years. One day, she'd be responsible for going through the items in the house when her mother passed away, and the thought made her want to cry.

"Oh, now it's not that bad. You know how I like to collect things." Edie Cole didn't collect things. She made messes and saved everything, but she was by no means a collector.

"But this place is so unsafe! There's mold in here and the smell is overwhelming, Mom. Why don't you let me help you get into a new place and get rid of all this stuff?" She didn't know why she was having this conversation. They had this conversation once a year, every year. And it never went anywhere good.

"You know, today is Mother's Day. Let's not have an argument, Kelly," she said in a very flat voice. Her mother had seemed devoid of emotion in recent years. Maybe it had been the years of drug abuse, or maybe she just didn't feel anything anymore. Kelly had found herself sharing that attribute at times, willing herself not to "feel" so as to avoid pain. Her entire childhood had been one painful day after another, mostly contained within the house where she currently stood, and the avoidance of feelings had served her well. Most of the time.

But it had also cost her dearly in the way of long-lasting friendships and love relationships. She was never able to get too close, unwilling to open herself to pain. As a child, she'd learned that trusting in someone meant pain, and now that she was an adult she could avoid most of that. She could choose her friends, choose those she allowed inside of her bubble, and choose who she trusted. Which was no one really. She trusted Maggie the most out of everyone she knew, but even that wasn't 100%.

And she had trusted her best friend, but that didn't turn out so well.

"Kelly, did you hear me?" her mother said, her tiny hand on her hip as she stared at Kelly with her hollowed out brown eyes.

"What?" Kelly responded, pulling herself out of her thoughts.

"Can we just not talk about the house today?"

"When can we talk about it, Mom? I see you once a year, and this just gets worse every time I come. Avoiding it isn't solving the problem," she said, running her fingers through her brown hair with a sigh.

"It's my house, and I'll not have you bullying me into getting rid of my collections." Her tone had changed, and Kelly knew that tone very well. It was stubbornness. She knew there was no sense in continuing the fight. She'd never win.

"Fine. What would you like to do then? We can go to Lyla's Tea Room, if you'd like."

"No, I don't want to go anywhere," Edie said.

"Mom, we can't stay here. Where will we sit? I'm not eating out of that kitchen," Kelly declared. She didn't care what her mother thought about that statement; she wasn't getting food poisoning.

"Then let's sit out back," Edie said as she turned and started climbing her way through the debris.

The backyard was the only area not overwhelmed with junk. Edie kept it fairly nice, with a few pots - that mostly had weeds in them - strewn about the small concrete slab. She had a couple of metal lawn chairs and a small glass top table sitting on the patio, all of which was mildewed from being out in the weather year-round. Still, it was a far cry better than the inside of the house.

Kelly sat down and looked out at the yard. Most kids had good memories of their yards growing up. All Kelly saw was space that had rarely been used. She'd had no father to toss the ball with her, no mother to teach her how to garden. Instead, they'd either been inside shooting heroin or snorting cocaine, or maybe on the patio smoking pot. It just depended on their moods at the time.

When she turned around, her mother was sitting in a plastic chair facing the yard. "Isn't it beautiful out here?" she said, a smile across her face as she stared.

She looked at her mother and realized that she wasn't like a normal person. The drugs had robbed her of normalcy long ago, and whatever she saw in the yard that she thought was beautiful, Kelly sure didn't see it.

What she saw were a bunch of weeds mixed in with what used to be grass. There were patches of mud throughout the yard, and weeds were growing over the fence line. But her mother saw something totally different, and maybe that was for the best.

Her mother's face had weathered more over the last twelve months. Kelly knew that she was aging, but it was much more accelerated due to her drug use in the past. It made her feel bad that she wasn't making more of an effort to see her mom, but the decision to see her only once a year have been a tough one.

In years past, Kelly allowed her mother's situation to infiltrate her own life. It had ruined jobs and relationships and Kelly's sense of peace in her own life. She worked very hard to create that peace, and she intended to maintain that no matter what.

Sometimes that meant getting rid of men she was dating or jobs that didn't serve her. It was like a life preserver. She had to have order and peace in her life to feel safe.

Her childhood had been anything but safe, but she tried not to focus on that. Instead, she focused on living her best life in the present. But lately she was wondering if that was really happening at all?

Breaking up with her last boyfriend had been difficult, for sure, but not necessarily for the reasons that everyone probably thought. She had liked Rio, but he wasn't her soulmate and she knew it. The reason their breakup had bothered her so much was because she felt like she was constantly going back to the beginning of a very long moving sidewalk. As soon as she almost got to the end of it, and thought she might be finding happiness for once, something would happen and she'd have to start all over again.

She was embarrassed. She knew her friends had to feel sorry for her, and that made her feel even worse. They were all getting married and having babies, and she was still standing at the other end of that sidewalk.

"Don't you think?" Her mother's voice interrupted her thoughts. Obviously, she had zoned out during a conversation she didn't know they were having.

"Don't I think what?" Kelly asked. Her mother shook her head and sighed.

"Are you even paying attention to me? I don't know why on earth you come to visit once a year if you're not even going to pay attention to me." Her mother's anger always seethed just beneath the surface. It had been a fixture in Kelly's childhood. Her mother's anger, her father's disinterest. It was a lethal combination for an adolescent psyche.

"Sorry, Mom, long drive. I just zoned out for a moment while I was looking at those beautiful butterflies on your bush over there." Kelly was always very good at coming up with something to answer when her mom asked a question. It was like she went on autopilot during these visits because it was the only way to survive. She'd gone on autopilot her entire growing up years, so it wasn't as difficult as one might think.

"I was saying that the fence looks lovely with the vines growing on it." Kelly looked again at the fence line. It was covered in weeds, not vines. It was just nature taking over, not a beautiful piece of horticulture.

"Of course," she said, unwilling to get in an argument over weeds growing on the fence.

"Are you hungry?" her mother asked. There wasn't any way on God's green earth she was eating something from that kitchen, so she simply shook her head no.

"Not really. I had a late breakfast. Are you hungry?" Carrying on this conversation was becoming tedious. She felt bad, but if her mom didn't want to leave the house and they couldn't sit inside, it was clear that this was going to be a very short visit.

"Kind of, but I have a can of chili in there that I'm going to eat when you leave." Now it was even clearer that her mother didn't expect her to stay very long. Suddenly, it occurred to Kelly that maybe her mother didn't want this visit any more than she did. Perhaps they at least had that in common.

"Mom, I don't know what to say to you. I really… I don't understand your lifestyle…" Kelly found herself stammering. She didn't even know what she was trying to say. She just felt like there was this huge elephant in the room that she needed to address.

"Kelly, I understand that you don't like my life-style, but I'm happy. I like my life. If you can't accept that, I can't help you." That was the most coherent her mother had ever sounded in recent years. Was it possible that she really did like living like this? How can anyone want to live around mounds of trash and junk? Kelly would never understand it, but her mother was right. She had the right to live exactly the way she wanted. Thank goodness her house had been paid for, or she probably would've already been out on the streets. Certainly no landlord would accept the way the house looked.

"I'm just concerned about your safety. The place is so packed that if one thing caught on fire, it's going to burn down around you. What if you have a heart attack and you fall out in the floor? How in the world are the paramedics going to get to you? Or even find you?" she said.

It really was frustrating for Kelly. She loved her mother, but not in the way most people loved their mothers. But she still felt a sense of responsibility, and her hands were completely tied in the situation. There was always the option of trying to get her mother declared mentally unstable, but she really wasn't. She took care of herself as best as could be expected under the circumstances.

"Listen, if those things happen then I reckon it's

in God's will. I'm not going to worry about it. This is the way I live, Kelly, and that's not going to change. You've always been like this!" Her mother stared at her with a look of ferocity that she remembered from her childhood.

"Been like what?"

"Tightly wound. That's what my grandmother would've called it," her mother said raising her eyebrows. "You need to learn to chill out. Do you have a man yet?" Kelly simultaneously wanted to slap her mother and start crying.

"Mom, I'm tightly wound because I've had to be. Look how I grew up. Someone had to be the adult." She'd never said something like that to her mother before.

"Enough. If you want to talk like that, then leave."

It was the final word on the subject, at least for this year, and Kelly decided that it was better not to continue the argument.

They spent the next half hour in companionable silence as they looked out over the yard and listened to the birds chirp off in the distance.

It had always been amazing to Kelly that she could hear such beautiful sounds while terrible things were going on. When she was a child, she'd sit by her bedroom window listening to the birds chirp in the neighbor's birdfeeder while her parents yelled at each other in the other room. It was like she was always reaching out for that one little morsel of peace in her crazy world.

It was no wonder that she had to keep such a tight hold on organization and serenity now.

And then she thought about that stupid karate school that had moved in upstairs at her beloved spa. What was she going to do about that?

* * *

MOTHER'S DAY had really taken it out of Kelly. She only spent one hour with her mother after driving two hours to get there, but she was so ready to leave. At least she kept in touch with her mother occasionally by text and email, but their worlds just didn't intersect as often as a normal mother/daughter relationship would.

Still, every Mother's Day left Kelly feeling emotionally drained. Trying to deal with her mother had been difficult for her whole life, and she had hoped that maybe that would change once she had been clean from drugs for a while. Instead, she simply replaced one habit with another. Hoarding was her new love, and Kelly still didn't compare. She could never compete with drugs and alcohol, and now she could never compete with hoarding.

CHAPTER 4

She drove up the next morning to the spa, her respite from the crazy world, and parked her car next to some motorcycle that had now appeared in the parking lot. She knew it wasn't Maggie's, but now she shared the building with Mr. Karate, so maybe it was his.

Kelly had given Maggie the day off since she went to visit her mother in a neighboring county. Maggie had a great relationship with her mom, something Kelly envied for sure. At least she would have a few hours alone. She had canceled appointments for the morning time so she could get caught up on some things before afternoon clients arrived.

She walked in the door, turned on the lights and went into her office. Although she loved the old building, it could be lonely in times like this when there were no clients or coworkers to talk to. Kelly had to admit that her life was a bit lonelier lately than she would've liked.

Of course, some of that was her own doing. She'd closed herself off for so long that it was hard to let other people in.

Realizing that she wanted to make the week as good as it could be, she decided that the best way to start it would be with meditation. Kelly love to meditate and do yoga. Sometimes, it was the only thing that kept her from going insane.

She put her purse down in the office and walked into the room where yoga classes were held. It was an open space with hardwood floors and mirrors lining one wall. One day, she planned to have Pilates classes and maybe even some dance classes in there if she could find a teacher to rent the space to.

Cat was a wonderful yoga teacher, but she came with her own brand of insanity and constant relationship woes herself. In fact, she didn't really know of anyone around her that had a good relationship right now. Maybe something was in the water.

She turned on a small lamp in the corner of the room and sat down on the floor. Sitting up and putting the bottoms of her feet together, she took in several deep breaths to center herself. Deep breathing always helped her in times of crisis. She'd used it a lot as a child.

When she was finally calmed down, she laid on the floor, legs and arms spread as far out as they would go, much like she was doing a snow angel. She found that getting in the most comfortable position for meditation allowed her mind to clear. And getting a clear mind was extremely important to her. Otherwise, she lived in chaos and that was something she tried to avoid at all costs.

She continued taking deep breaths, allowing them to come in and out at their own pace. Meditation had been something she had learned over the years because she was a type A personality with a very active imagination. Shutting that down for any length of time had been a challenge at first, but she eventually got the hang of using her own method of meditation.

Just as her mind cleared, and probably a few minutes into meditation, she felt someone shaking her violently.

"Are you okay? Wake up! Wake up!" the man yelled. Kelly opened her eyes, hazy as they were, and noticed Quinn Maverick kneeling over her.

"What are you doing?" she yelled at him as she sat up and accidentally bumped heads with him.

Quinn stood up and held his forehead, a look of confusion and then irritation on his face.

"I thought something was wrong! Who just comes in and lays on the floor?"

"Someone who's meditating!" she said as she stood to her feet. "And who starts shaking someone violently that they barely know?"

"Well, excuse me for trying to help. I thought something was wrong, like maybe you passed out or something."

"Haven't you ever seen anyone meditate before? Do you think I would've come in and turned on the lamp before I randomly passed out?"

Quinn turned and looked at the small lamp lit up in the corner. He sighed, shook his head and chuckled.

"I guess not, but I didn't really have time to think about that. All I saw was a woman laying on the floor. I can't help myself. If I see someone I think is in trouble, I have to try to help them."

For a moment, something tugged at her heart-strings and she wasn't sure what it was. There was just something about this guy, aside from his ruggedly handsome good looks. He seemed like one of those knight in shining armor kind of guys who was always trying to sweep in and help some poor, pathetic woman. And then she started to get irritated.

"Well, I didn't need your help. I realize you're all martial arts, karate, save the world kind of stuff, but I can take care of myself, Mr. Maverick."

At the same time she said the words, she started

to hate herself a little. Here was this guy trying to help her, and she wanted to punch him in the nose for it. Even she didn't understand herself sometimes.

"Well, I'll be sure to keep that in mind in the future. You can slip down the stairs and bump your head or have a heart attack out in the parking lot, but I won't bother you. I'll make sure that you get your peace and quiet and meditation time," he said sarcastically.

With that, he turned and walked back up the stairs from where he'd apparently come. She hadn't even heard him, already deep into her meditation apparently.

Kelly stood in the empty room for a moment realizing what she'd done. Perhaps she was too hard on the man. Perhaps?

Suddenly, she realized that she probably was way too hard on a perfect stranger who was only trying to help. But she still couldn't bring herself to go upstairs and thank the man who was causing so much ruckus and noise when she was trying to run her quiet spa business.

Instead, she decided that working with this person in such close quarters just wasn't going to be an option. She had to do something to get him to move his business, so she opted to do the only thing she knew. It was time to call the landlord.

A few minutes later, Kelly was searching through

her phone for the landlord's number. She'd dealt with the landlord for two years now, and they had a great relationship as far as landlords and tenants went.

She didn't know how she was going to convince this woman, who obviously needed the money, to kick out a perfectly good tenant. Maybe she could use reverse psychology or extortion, she thought laughing.

"Helen? Hi, it's Kelly Cole from The Spirit Spa. Listen, we need to talk about something."

"Okay. What's going on?"

"Well, as you know I just came back from an extended trip, and I met my new upstairs neighbor," Kelly said, trying to start out slowly.

"You did? Well, that's good. Mr. Maverick is a wonderful person, and I know he's going to be a wonderful tenant as well." This was going to be harder than Kelly thought.

"Yes, he seems like a perfectly nice gentleman. But I do have some concerns..." Kelly said.

"Concerns?"

"Well, yes. First of all, the volume level of his classes is really interrupting the flow of my business. You know that my clients love the quiet serenity of the spa."

"Well, I can understand that. But there's nothing in your lease that says I can provide you with a 100% quiet..." Helen said.

"Two. I wasn't expecting to come back from vacation and find this sort of business just above mine. Also, the parking situation is becoming quite difficult."

"Really? Remember that both of you can also utilize the side yard. That will give you at least five or six more parking spaces."

"That is also true..." Kelly said, running out of ammunition. What was she going to say that was going to get this woman to break? "Listen, Helen, I'm going to be honest with you. If we can't resolve the situation, I'm going to have to start looking for another location at the end of my lease." Kelly knew she didn't mean it, but she had to try something. There had to be something that would get this guy kicked out of the building so that she could go back to enjoying a peaceful life.

"Well I'm sorry to hear that, Kelly, because you're such a great tenant. But I need the money, quite honestly. I'm taking care of my elderly mother, who has Alzheimer's, and the upstairs had been empty for so long that it just about made me go bankrupt. And if I go bankrupt, I lose the building which means you lose your space too." There was an eerie silence. Kelly could totally understand what was going on, and she couldn't really argue with it. Dang it. Plus her lease went for three more years.

"I'm so sorry to hear about your mother, Helen. I understand. We'll make it work. Don't worry about it," Kelly said before saying her goodbyes and hanging up. She was stuck with Quinn Maverick, and a part of her was irritated by it. But she was much more irritated by the fact that another part of her was a little bit excited to know that she got to look at him every day.

CHAPTER 5

*D*ragging herself up the stairs, Kelly decided that the only option she had was to apologize for her overreaction and try to make peace with Quinn. She was obviously going to have to share the space for the foreseeable future, at least until she could grow her business such that she could buy her own building. It was a dream, but something she held onto as a personal goal.

She walked quietly up the stairs, in her bare feet, and realized that his lights were out. She knew he hadn't left, so he must've been somewhere in the string of rooms that dotted the upstairs.

When she walked around the corner of one of the rooms, she could hear low music playing. She peeked through the cracked door, eavesdropping completely, and saw him sitting in a chair facing the window to the side yard with a guitar on his lap. He was strumming it quietly, humming something, and the whole sight was making her stomach tense up. Who was this guy? Rough one minute, soft the next. She'd never met anyone quite like him.

She took a moment to just look at him. He was probably the most handsome man she'd ever seen. She didn't use the word handsome a whole lot. Many guys were good-looking, hot, fine, sexy. And he was definitely sexy too, but he was handsome. Like an old Hollywood movie star, but a little rougher around the edges.

He had broad shoulders that she could see beneath the black T-shirt he was wearing. He had on windbreaker pants that were black with a white line down each side. His karate uniform, whatever it was called, was hanging in the corner, completely pressed and ironed.

On the back of the uniform she could see that he was a world champion, which didn't surprise her. She had seen him doing some kicks and punches and stretches the other day, and it was impressive. She had to at least admit that.

Still, the thought of a bunch of men and women beating each other to a pulp seemed stupid. She knew it was an age-old tradition, but she didn't really understand it that much.

She stepped a couple of inches closer so she could try to hear what song he was playing when one of the old hardwood floor pieces squeaked under her foot. He jumped, startled of course, and turned around making eye contact with her. Kelly started to flush red, even through her normally pale toned skin.

"I'm... I'm sorry..." she said, stammering out of sheer anxiety. She hated being caught doing anything she wasn't supposed to be doing.

"Can I help you with something?" he said, irritation coloring his voice.

"Can I come in?" she asked.

"You kind of already have," he said with a bit of a smirk on his face. He waved his hand for her to come in, put his guitar up against the window frame and stood. Dang. The muscles rippling under his shirt were making her mouth start to water, something she would never admit out loud.

She stepped forward into the room, and he turned on the light. It was one of those lights that hung down from the ceiling with a metal chain attached to it, obviously something that hadn't been updated by the landlord since buying the place.

"I just wanted to come up and say that I'm really sorry that I overreacted. I realize it probably looked like something bad had happened to me, lying on the floor all sprawled out like that. It wasn't your fault. It's just been tough few weeks for me. Let's just say I haven't been at my best."

He looked at her for a moment, a hint of a smile playing across his lips. Those full lips. What must they taste like? She mentally slapped herself to get her own attention again.

"I understand. I've had a lot of hard times myself lately. I really wasn't trying to offend you. I thought something had happened and when I think something has happened to someone, I try to help. But I'll be more careful from now on knowing that you meditate."

"Okay. Thanks. Look, we obviously have to share the space, and I'll try to be more understanding of the fact that your student group is a little more verbose."

"Verbose?"

"Yes. Sorry. It means…"

"I know what verbose means. I graduated from college, although that might be hard to believe," he said with a grin.

"Of course. I'm sorry. I didn't mean to…" She found herself stammering again.

"No big deal. People often misjudge me. If there's nothing else, I have some things to do," he said, ushering her toward the door. And she found herself hating him all over again.

* * *

AFTER WORKING HER MORNING HOURS, Kelly went home for lunch break. It was a dreary day, much more overcast than would be expected in the middle of May. And it was a greatly affecting her mood.

She decided to go home and try to get a few things done before heading back for her busy afternoon schedule. There were facials and massages and of course, Cat's yoga class. She thought seriously about participating to try to burn off some of the stress built up from visiting her mother.

Her cell phone rang as she walked in the door and put her purse on the kitchen counter. She looked down, but didn't immediately recognize the number so she answered it.

"Hello?"

"Oh, Kelly. Hello, love," the man said. She immediately recognized the voice as that of Rio's. What on earth was he doing calling her? The fact that he was calling her "love" meant nothing. He was a Casanova at the core, and he called everyone that.

"Rio. What on earth could you be calling me for? Aren't you living it up in Hawaii with your new girlfriend?" she said, the sarcasm and irritation evident in her voice.

"Kelly, don't be angry with me. I'm calling to check on you and make sure that you're doing okay. How goes everything?" he said, his broken English much more disgusting to her now.

"I'm not your problem anymore, Rio. And you can tell Abigail the same thing. Goodbye," she said before hanging up. The nerve of some people!

She decided that she needed something a little stiffer than coffee, but didn't drinking wine in the middle of the afternoon make her sad and pathetic? Of course, that wasn't a problem because she was feeling pretty sad and pathetic right now anyway.

She reached into the cabinet and grabbed a wine glass and found an almost empty bottle of wine left over in the refrigerator from the last time she and Rio went on a date. Good wine doesn't go bad that quickly, right? She didn't care. She wasn't exactly a wine connoisseur and didn't really care if it tasted good. Right now she was just in search of alcohol to numb the pain a little bit.

A couple of hours later, she was pulling back into the parking lot, ready to work. She had taken a hot bath, her second of the day, and drank a glass of wine. It was ecstasy. Well, the only kind of ecstasy she was going to feel for a long time.

When she pulled into the parking lot, it was sheer mayhem. Cat was standing beside her car, her hands up in the air in exasperation because someone had parked too close to her. Kelly got out of her car and started walking towards her.

"What's wrong?" Kelly asked.

"These karate parents are crazy!" Cat said. "This sadistic soccer mom pulled right beside my car, looked at me and went inside. Can you believe that crap?" For a yoga teacher, she was anything but serene. Cat was feisty, sexy and outspoken. It was probably a lot of the reason why she couldn't keep a man.

"I know. This is ridiculous. I talked to the landlord and she said we could use the side yard for few more parking spaces, but I don't think that's going to be enough. Maybe she didn't have any idea how many clients he really had, but I can't talk her into cutting his lease."

"Cutting my lease?" she heard Quinn Maverick say from behind her. What was he doing in the parking lot?

"Mr. Maverick..."

"Please, call me Quinn. After all, if you're going to talk about me behind my back, we should at least be on a first name basis." The smirk on his face made her want to slap him, then kiss him and then slap him some more.

"I wasn't trying to talk behind your back."

"Well, it sure seems that way. Anyway, I can't believe you would call the landlord and try to get my lease canceled. That's a pretty crappy thing to do." He started to walk past her but she snapped.

"Wait just a minute!" she said. "You came into *my* territory. Before you got here, we had plenty of parking and plenty of quiet. Now we have to deal with all the noise and the stomping and the shouting and the parking situation..." she said, the wine having worn off and the hot bath having not been enough.

He stopped and turned, smiling. "I guess our little cease-fire is over? Either way, you don't have to like that I'm here. But you do have to accept it because I have a legal right to be here. In fact, it's just as much of a legal right as you have. So unless you want to cut your own lease, I suggest you leave mine alone. Good evening, ladies," he said as he walked off and up the stairs into the building.

"Gosh, he's so hot," Cat said, practically purring again.

"Really? He's a jerk. He's a complete and utter waste of space, and I can't stand him!" Kelly said as she started to walk towards the building.

"Methinks the lady doth protest too much!" Cat called to her. Kelly was not as surprised by the quote as she was to the fact that Cat knew anything about Shakespeare.

CHAPTER 6

*K*elly didn't have children yet, but she was quite sure Quinn Maverick operated like one. Fairly quiet most of the day, but as the evening arrived he got louder and louder.

He was so loud that she was learning a lot of new Korean words just listening to him teach classes upstairs. The stomping and yelling was almost too much to take. Her serenity was broken now, and she was sure her clients would start leaving soon.

Only, that wasn't happening. Over the last few days, some of them had come and signed their children up for karate classes. A few of the fathers, who never came into the spa but paid for their wives to enjoy its services, had signed up too. Midlife crisis much?

Yep, Quinn must have been a good salesman too. She imagined that he probably sold women that way too. He probably had all kinds of dates every night of the week, feeding women lines to get them to do what he wanted. Of course, she had nothing to base this on, but it was fun to think about while she stewed over how much she despised him.

As she sat in her office, waiting for Cat to finish her evening classes, she wondered if she would always be alone. Always the one without kids, without a husband or even an ex-husband. Some of her friends were already on their second marriage. She was so behind.

She could hear Maggie's voice echoing in her ear. "You know, online dating has worked for a lot of my friends…" she would say, often, in her sing songy little voice.

"Mags, I don't have any interest in meeting some loser who's probably sitting on his sofa in his sweat pants eating a pint of ice cream."

Lately, she realized that she was, in fact, that loser.

The laptop was sitting open in front of her, practically calling her name. Surely there were no eligible bachelors she didn't know already in Whiskey Ridge. Everybody knew everybody else in the town. Online dating couldn't possibly work for her simply on that basis alone.

But, it didn't stop her from filling out a profile and taking a selfie before she could talk herself out of it. And it didn't stop her from clicking "publish" on said profile. And it certainly didn't stop her from sitting there, second guessing what she'd just done and feeling a bit nauseous.

Even still, she closed the laptop and smiled. At least she had done something to move her life forward.

* * *

IT WASN'T twenty-four hours later when Kelly received her first response on her dating profile. Honestly, she thought it would be sooner than that, so she was starting to feel like the girl in school who never gets asked to the dance.

The guy looked nice enough. Sandy brown hair, a chiseled jawline, blue eyes. He was wearing a blue sweater in his photo which meant it ether wasn't all that recent or he hadn't gotten the memo that spring was here.

He lived two counties over, closer to the metro Atlanta area, but it was still only about an hour drive for him to come see her. His profile said he was in school to become a pharmacist and that he loved dogs and Chinese food. Hopefully not together, she thought.

"Hi, Kelly. I read your profile, and it sounds like we have a lot in common. Want to chat sometime?"

That was it. Simple, to the point. Normal.

For some reason, it didn't really resonate with

her, but maybe she could use him as practice, whatever that meant. She messaged back:

"Hi, Peter. Nice to virtually meet you. I'd love to chat sometime. Here's my number..."

Peter called six minutes later. It made her a little uneasy to think he was desperate, but he explained that he was studying for his finals and saw her message pop up on his computer while he was doing some research. He welcomed the break, or at least that's how he explained the quick callback.

Of course, what guy is going to fess up and say, "No one wants to date me, so when I saw your message I pounced like a puma on a bunny rabbit"? Do pumas even eat rabbits?

They talked for about half an hour and planned a date for the weekend. She wasn't really nervous, but she wasn't overly excited either. Hopefully he was more on the boring end of the spectrum and not on the ax murderer end of it.

The plan was to meet at Leighton's, one of the snazzier restaurants in town. Just off the main square, the restaurant was built inside of an old mill and had high-class Southern cuisine. She'd only been there once because it was pretty expensive, but Peter found it online and asked if they could meet there.

So far, so good. At the very least, maybe it would get the sexy Quinn Maverick's face... and other parts... out of her mind for awhile.

She'd never admit it out loud, but seeing him day

in and day out was proving to be difficult. The man was sexy. There was no getting around it. The stay-at-home mothers were flocking to the place, signing their munchkins up by the droves, just so they could stare at him.

And she couldn't blame them.

But he was also her arch nemesis right now. She couldn't give in, and this Peter guy was the perfect diversion. He was handsome, in a "bring him home to your mother and your grandma" kind of way.

Sure, being a "pharmacy student" wasn't nearly as sexy as being a "super ninja black belt smoking-hot karate instructor" was, but beggars couldn't be choosers at this point.

"So, wait, let me get this straight. The super serious and always careful Kelly Cole is going on a date with a perfect stranger tonight?" Maggie said when Friday finally arrived on the calendar.

"Don't pick at me," Kelly warned as she closed her laptop and prepared to head home to get ready. She was leaving early, for once.

"I think it's great. Ask if he has a brother," Maggie said with a giggle. "A sexy, tall brother with a fat bank account and a tight butt."

Leave it to Maggie to make her laugh when she was getting more nervous by the second. "If he has one of those, I call dibs on him."

Kelly drove home and did what all women do before a date. She chose the perfect outfit - a pair of white capri pants and a red flowy top - and tamed her unruly hair. With a bit of makeup to jazz up her normally natural look, she was ready to go.

The drive to Leighton's was short, but every drive in Whiskey Ridge was short. You could practically throw a baseball from one end of the town to the other. Well, maybe that was over-exaggerating things a bit, but it was close to the truth.

"Kelly?" Peter said as she walked into the front door at Leighton's. Boy, he was as punctual as anyone she'd ever met, especially since they weren't supposed to meet for another fifteen minutes.

But she was early too, so what did that say about her?

He was taller than she'd imagined, probably at least six feet. He wore a pair of beige slacks, a button up white shirt and a red tie. She half expected him to wait the tables rather than sit at one.

"Hi. Nice to meet you," she said, accepting the small bouquet of flowers he'd brought for her. Nice touch. "Oh, thanks so much for the flowers…" she barely got out before the inevitable sneezing fit started.

"You okay?" he asked.

"All….er…gies…" she managed to say between sneezes. Yep. She was highly allergic to flowers, especially when someone placed them directly near her face.

"Oh my gosh. I'm so sorry… I had no idea…" he

stammered as he grabbed the bouquet from her and managed to then cut her hand with one of the rose thorns.

Blood pooled in the palm of her hand as she continued sneezing in the waiting area of the posh restaurant. People were starting to stare, and her watering eyes made it appear as if she was crying.

Perfect first date.

"It's okay," she finally managed to say after the manager gave her some tissue. And a Band-Aid. And a Benadryl pill from the first aid kit.

Note to self: Don't drink wine tonight or else you might fall asleep at the table.

When they were finally seated at a table in the back corner - probably not an accident on the part of the staff at Leighton's - she smiled.

"I'm so embarrassed. I've never had such a quick reaction like that before..." The palm of her hand continued to throb in her lap, but at least her sinuses were starting to reopen.

"I wish I'd known you were allergic," he said, a little bit of irritation evident in his voice. Who could blame him? He probably spent a small fortune on those flowers, and they were now sitting in a vase on the bar. At least Leighton's could make use of them.

"Didn't think to add it to my profile," she mumbled back before looking down at the menu.

Dinner went better than their first meeting, but not by much. Peter talked of pharmacy school mostly, explaining all of his classes in exhausting detail which would make him a great and accurate pharmacist but a particularly dull conversationalist.

He drank - a lot - at dinner. A couple of beers, a glass of wine and some mixed drink. Kelly didn't mind people drinking socially, but after growing up with her substance abusing parents, she didn't like to be around anyone who overindulged.

Once dessert and coffee were served, Kelly had her mind on one thing. She wanted to go home, put on her bathrobe and cuddle with Tux in the recliner. Yep, living the dream.

There definitely wouldn't a second date with this guy, but up until that point he'd done nothing particularly wrong. He just wasn't particularly right for her.

"Care to take a walk?" he asked as they crossed through the doorway and out onto the sidewalk.

"Um…"

"Come on. We had a bit of a rough beginning, but I've enjoyed talking to you. Even if we just become friends, can't we all use more friends?" Even as he asked her, she could hear his speech slurring, and it suddenly dawned on her that she didn't want to be responsible for him driving drunk and killing someone.

Visions of the makeshift memorial in front of her house flitted through her mind. Even though that accident probably wasn't caused by alcohol, she still knew how devastating car accidents could be.

So, basically, taking a walk with an intoxicated, boring pharmacy student was possible saving a life. Dang it.

"Okay. Sure," she said.

They walked for about ten minutes before she started noticing something. He was inching ever closer to her. First, his hand brushed hers, so she swiftly stuck both of her hands into her tiny capri pant pockets. But that didn't stop the invasion of space.

"Hey, maybe we should walk the square," she finally said as they passed the small Baptist church in town and the adjoining old cemetery that always creeped her out.

"Nah, that sounds boring," he said, his speech still slurring. "Let's sit." He pointed to a park bench in front of the church, and then sat down before she had a chance to agree or disagree. Maybe he needed to sit down more than she didn't want to sit down.

"Okay, for a minute. But then I think we should get you a cup of coffee."

He slid his arm up around and behind her, and she didn't resist because at least he wasn't actually touching her. The fact that there was literally nobody around was starting to concern her, though. If this guy was on the ax murderer end of the spectrum, he could kill her right here and bury her in the creepy cemetery before anyone was the wiser.

Maybe that was stretching the truth a bit.

And then he did it. "The lean". The "I'm going to try to kiss you with my alcohol tinged lips even though you've given me no reason to believe you want to kiss me" lean.

Kelly jumped upright and stepped two feet back, almost falling off the curb in the process.

"What are you doing?" she yelled.

"Oh come on, you know you want it," he slurred. How did he seem to be getting drunker by the minute? Did he have a flask hidden somewhere?

"I can assure you, I don't want 'it' or anything else from you," she said. "I'm leaving."

Kelly hurriedly walked toward civilization, or at least what passed as civilization in Whiskey Ridge. She could see the lights in the center of the square. If she could just get there…

"Woman, don't run away from me." The anger in his voice as he grabbed her by her shoulder and twirled her around was frightening and reminded her of her father.

"Let go of me!" she screamed as loud as she could, but the dang train that ran just outside of town muffled her voice.

He had both of her arms now, attempting to pull her closer and force her to kiss him when suddenly his grasp on her arms was gone. And then he was on the ground out cold, blood at the corner of his lips.

What had just happened? Had he passed out right in the middle of attacking her? And why was his lip bleeding?

It took just a few seconds to come to her senses and realize what was going on.

"Are you okay?"

She turned to see Quinn standing beside her rubbing the knuckles on his right hand. He stood with an intensity she hadn't seen before, leaning toward her, concern on his face. She sucked in a sharp breath, unsure of what to say so she opted instead to answer his question.

"I'm fine."

Peter finally roused on the ground enough to let Kelly know he was still alive. "Who is this guy?"

"He was my... date." Kelly was turning all shades of red at the thought of being on a date with such an obvious loser.

"Not many other prospects?" Quinn said, sarcasm evident in his words.

"Do you have to be such a jerk all the time?"

"You realize you're the only one who thinks that about me, don't you?"

She found that incredibly hard to believe. "I didn't need your help, you know."

"Well, you certainly looked like you did," he said as he bent down and dragged Peter's mostly lifeless body onto the sidewalk. Moments later, a police car drove by and Quinn explained the situation to the officer. They loaded Peter into the car, took statements from Kelly and Quinn and took him to the drunk tank. Kelly didn't press charges.

As all of the businesses in town closed their doors for the night, Kelly started walking toward her home. Quinn jogged to catch up with her.

"Woman, are you crazy?" he said when he finally caught her.

"Excuse me?"

"You were just attacked, and now you're walking home in the dark alone?"

"Listen, Maverick, I don't need a knight in shining armor, okay?"

"Well, you seemed to need one back there."

"He was drunk. I could've handled him," she said as she continued walking. "Plus, I know this town inside and out. I know every person in it, and I'm not scared to be walking home in the dark alone."

"False sense of security," he said. "You need to be trained."

"Pardon?" Kelly said, stopping short and causing him to run into her.

"I teach self defense techniques to women just for this reason."

"Oh, no no no... Not happening..." She continued walking, determined to leave him in the dust.

"Why not?" He fell back in step with her.

"Because I don't want to be one of those people who is scared of everything and constantly looking over my shoulder. I live in a small town America for a reason."

"People who know how to defend themselves don't look over their shoulders."

"I said no," she repeated as she kept walking.

"Okay, fine. But can I ask you a question?" She stopped and turned to him, her arms crossed.

"What?"

"Explain to me, just so I can sleep tonight, what you would've done if he'd dragged you into the woods over there."

"Alright... I would've kicked him in the crotch."

"Seriously?"

"Sure. Any self-respecting woman would've done the same."

"And you'd be dead right now. If kicking men in the crotch worked, no woman would ever be kidnapped or killed."

He had a point.

"Fine. Tell me about your classes," she finally relented as they started walking again.

67

Kelly wanted to be anywhere but here. Standing in her yoga pants and t-shirt in the middle of the floor of a karate studio was not her idea of a good time.

Only one other woman was there, and she was as old as the hills. Kelly had no idea why she was taking a self-defense class at her age, and she was scared that if they had to work with each other she might break one of the woman's bones accidentally. And then there were would be a lawsuit and an appearance on Judge Judy…

"Okay, ladies. I'm Master Maverick," Quinn started. Kelly immediately giggled, and he didn't look amused at all.

"Miss Cole, is something funny?"

"Master Maverick. Just sounds… like a cartoon character or something." She held her hand over her mouth, trying desperately to contain herself. The warning look he gave her was a bit unnerving, but he continued.

"Anyway, you're both here today to learn some maneuvers to protect yourselves in the event that someone tries to attack you. This class is six weeks long, and we'll meet twice a week..."

Six weeks? Twice a week? He hadn't mentioned the huge time commitment to her. She just wanted to learn how to kick butt and take names, but she didn't want to make a career of it.

"Twelve classes?" Kelly finally blurted out after he'd started teaching the actual class.

"Yes, Miss Cole," he said, glaring at her again.

After doing some warm ups, which included jumping jacks and squats, they got started on some of the techniques.

"The first move I want to demonstrate involves someone grabbing you from behind, around your neck. Miss Cole, come on up and let me demonstrate," he said. She froze in place. Physical contact with Quinn Maverick was about to take place. Maybe she hadn't thought this through enough.

She slowly walked to the front. He moved behind her, his chest up against her back as he slid his arm around her neck, her chin firmly against the crook of his elbow. It was uncomfortable in a multitude of different ways.

First of all, my dear God, his chest muscles were

heavenly. She could feel them against her back, flexing and moving as he breathed.

Second of all, he smelled like all the good things in life rolled into one. Cologne. Sweat. Hard work. Maybe even puppies.

Third, she almost liked the way he was holding her, even though he was supposed to be an attacker. She stood there limp in his arms. It had been a very long time since a real man had held her.

"Um, Miss Cole, can you struggle… or something?" he whispered into her ear. His lips brushed against her earlobe and she went weak in the knees. This was ridiculous. He was just a man. A normal man. A ruggedly sexy normal man.

Imagine him pooping.

Yep, that was her "go to" answer to getting over crushes. Her mother had once told her to do that when she had a crush on a boy in high school that had no interest in her.

"Imagine him pooping," she'd said. "He's just like you and me. Everybody poops."

It might have worked in ninth grade, but right now the thought of Quinn pooping just made her want to buy a candle and sit next to him while he did it.

Dang.

"Struggle," Quinn whispered again. Mentally slapping herself, she pulled and struggled while he explained the maneuver that would save her from this kind of attack. At the end, she had not a clue what he'd said.

He wanted her to demonstrate it with the other woman in class, whose name turned out to be Clara, but they were both lost. Thankfully, Clara wasn't the top student in their little class, so she had no idea what was going on either.

When the hour was up, Kelly was ecstatic to get the heck out of there and made a beeline for the door, following Clara to the top of the stairs.

"Excuse me, Miss Cole?" Quinn called before she could make her full escape. She slowly turned, quite sure that her beet red face was going to give her away.

"Yes?" she said innocently.

"Are you okay? You seemed... dazed... during class."

"Sure. I'm fine," she said, turning again.

Then she felt his hand on her arm, a soft touch that she wasn't expecting.

"I just wanted to make sure I wasn't bringing up any bad memories or anything..." he said softly.

"Bad memories?"

"Well, a lot of women have had experiences. These classes can sometimes trigger certain memories..."

"Oh. No. Nothing like that. I was just a bit distracted, that's all."

"Good. Well, see you Thursday," he said before

turning and heading into his office. How was she going to make it another eleven classes with a man she was unquestionably attracted to but couldn't stand?

Ugh.

* * *

THURSDAY ROLLED AROUND FASTER than she'd expected, and she searched for ways to get out of class. But she couldn't. He'd already confirmed with her earlier in the day.

"Hey," she said as she walked into the studio. His previous class was walking out already, and he was taking off the top of his uniform. Yum.

"Hey, Miss Cole."

"Please, call me Kelly."

"Okay," he said, with just a hint of a smile as his eyes lingered on hers for a long moment. "Kelly, it is."

She put her purse in the corner of the room and silenced her phone. "Where's Clara?"

"Sick."

One word that threw her for a loop.

"So it's just me and you tonight?" she asked.

"I'm afraid so," he said as he closed the space between them. Self defense class was so… close.

"We can reschedule if you'd like…" she offered.

"No, of course not. I wouldn't want you out

walking the streets kicking guys in the crotch or something."

"Very funny."

"Okay, let's start tonight with the move I used to get the drunk guy on the ground…"

"You mean punching him in the mouth?" she asked with a smile.

"No, I mean after I punched him…" He was all business, showing her the exact process of taking someone down.

She practiced over and over with him until she was tired and the hour was already up. This time wasn't so bad. Maybe she would get used to this and could ignore his movie star appeal.

"Is that your phone I hear vibrating?" he asked as they finished up.

Kelly walked across the room and saw numerous missed calls lit up on the screen. They were all from some unknown number, but she did have a voicemail.

"Hi, Kelly. This is Estelle, your mother's neighbor. Listen, there's no easy way to say this and I wish I could talk to you in person, but your mother's house has burned to the ground. It's a total loss. You know how she is… with her possessions… and something caught a spark. She's okay. They took her to the ER as a precaution, but she really has nowhere to go, sweetie. I just can't have her stay here longterm. You know why… Call me…"

Kelly stood there with her mouth hanging open before accidentally dropping her phone on the hardwood floor.

"Hey, you okay?" Quinn asked, seeing her face in the mirrored wall, the color drained from her skin.

"Oh my God…" she said softly.

"What's wrong?" He held onto her arm as he spoke to her, obviously aware that she was on the verge of fainting.

"My mom…"

"Is she okay?" he asked, struggling to get her to look at him. Kelly pulled herself together quickly, as was her style, and took a deep breath. She stood upright and shook his hand away from her arm.

"Yes, she's fine. But I have an emergency so I need to get to Atlanta." She walked to the door and ran down the stairs with Quinn chasing after her, holding her purse.

"Kelly, hold up!" he called as she made a beeline for the parking lot.

Her small car sat under the shade tree at the corner of the lot. She opened the door and climbed inside, turning the key in the ignition before noticing Quinn standing there with her purse.

"Thanks," she muttered, desperate to get out of the situation quickly before she had to explain anything about her mother. But then the car wouldn't start. Not even a sound when she turned the key. "Dang it!"

"Calm down. It's probably the battery, or it might be the starter..."

"I don't have time for this!" She grabbed her phone and stepped out of the car, dialing the local car rental place. They'd closed an hour ago. She then dialed Maggie, but there was no answer. Then she remembered that Maggie was at her book club and often turned off her phone after work in the evenings.

"Kelly, tell me what's going on. Come on," Quinn said, touching her arm and forcing her to make eye contact. "I'd like to think we're at least becoming friends."

A small smile formed on her face at the thought of that. Right now, he was really her only hope anyway. Maybe he could get her car started or something.

"My mother's house burned to the ground. She's at the ER, and I need to go get her in Atlanta." She blurted it out quickly, the stress of her voice even surprising her.

"Let's go then," he said, pointing at his truck across the lot.

"What?"

"I'll take you to Atlanta. We'll pick up your mother and bring her back tonight."

"Absolutely not!" Kelly said before sitting back down in her car and repeatedly trying to crank it.

"Kelly, what other choice do you have?"

"I'm not asking a stranger to drive me two hours away and pick up my mother."

"I'm not a stranger," he said with a laugh. "I saved you, remember?"

"Oh dear God. You did not 'save' me." She used air quotes like a cliche teenager.

"Whatever. Either way, I don't see what your other option would be. I'm here, I'm free and I'm willing." Kelly almost laughed at the way he said it, but decided the time wasn't appropriate.

"Okay," she finally relented. What other choice did she have? He was right. Her ultimate goal was to get to her mother, make sure she was okay and bring her back to Whiskey Ridge.

The thought of that turned her stomach. She couldn't let her mother live with her. There was no way. Her home was her sanctuary, and she was an organized person. Type A. Everything had to be in its place.

Her mother would destroy her life just like she had as a kid.

Thinking that way made her feel incredibly guilty, but truth was truth. She couldn't let her mother ruin her whole life yet again.

After locking up, Quinn walked her to his truck and opened the passenger door for her. A momentary thought flitted through her mind of the fact that Rio had never once opened a door, any door, for her.

"So, where to exactly?" Quinn asked as they

pulled out of the parking lot. It had just started to get dark outside, but it would be pitch black by the time they reached the hospital.

"Just get me to I-85 and I'll direct you from there," she said, buckling her seatbelt and looking down at her phone. She dialed Estelle's number.

"Hello?" the older woman said, sounding as if she had already been asleep. It was only a little before eight o'clock, for goodness sakes.

"Mrs. Goodwin, this is Kelly Cole."

"Oh, hello, Kelly. Thank goodness you called. Your mother is having fits at the hospital. You know, my granddaughter, Olivia, she works at the hospital as a nurse. Says your momma is yelling at the staff and wanting to go home..."

Kelly had to interrupt her. Estelle was known for her sharp tongue and fast talking. "I'm so sorry to hear that," she said over her. "I'm on my way. Can you let your daughter know?"

"Sure, honey. Will do," Estelle said before hanging up the phone without warning. The woman must have been eighty years old now, but she sure didn't sound like it.

They rode in companionable silence for awhile before Quinn finally started talking.

"So, your mom lives in Atlanta but you live in Whiskey Ridge. Any reason why?"

"Are people supposed to live near their mommies their whole lives?" she asked. "Or is it because I'm a woman that I'm expected to care for my mother no matter what I want?"

"You're like talking to a porcupine sometimes," he said, shaking his head.

"Talk to a lot of porcupines, do you?" she muttered under her breath.

"Why don't you like me?" he asked. She could see a quirk of a smile in his silhouette against the growing darkness outside.

"Never said I didn't like you."

"But you don't. I'm a pretty good judge of people, and you definitely don't like me."

She sighed. She was tired of fighting this guy. "Well, I like peace and quiet and order. Your business has completely wrecked that for me and my customers."

"Really? Have you paid attention lately? I mean really paid attention?"

"What do you mean?"

"Kelly, your customers are joining my classes. The moms of my students are coming downstairs during class and taking yoga at your place. Several have had massages or facials. Have you looked at your books? I think my business has actually added to your bottom line."

She wanted to argue, but now that she thought about it, he might be right. Dang it.

"I liked the silence," she said softly.

"Then maybe that says something about you and not me."

"Excuse me?" she said, turning in her seat and crossing her arms.

"Well, pardon me for saying so, but what I see is this beautiful young woman who's walling herself off to the world for some reason. There's enough time for silence when we're dead. Life's for the living."

"Did you buy a quote book or something?" she asked, rolling her eyes and turning back to face the front.

And then she remembered he'd called her beautiful.

"And the sarcasm... Jeez... sometimes people are just trying to help you. Don't be so defensive."

"Any other personality traits I should work on?" she asked, pretending to take notes on her phone. "Do I smell?"

"Yes."

"What?" she asked with a laugh.

"You smell... like lilies and lilacs and roses all mixed together." He said it so low she almost didn't hear it. And then she ignored it.

"So, what brought you to Whiskey Ridge, Mr. Question Asker?"

All of the sudden he got quiet. There was an air of discomfort in the car, almost darker than the night sky. She heard him swallow, hard, before he started to answer.

"My wife died."

Her heart sank. She felt so bad for him. For snapping at him. For being sarcastic.

"I'm so sorry, Quinn."

"We were married for five years. She died a little over a year ago."

"So you came here to… start over?"

"Kind of, I guess. I had a karate studio in Tennessee, so it just made sense to start one when I got to Whiskey Ridge. It's what I know how to do, and it's what I love. It's helped me start to heal."

"I understand. What was her name?"

"Penny."

"Penny," she repeated. She wanted to ask how she died, but she stopped short since it was really none of her business at all. They were just small talking, not giving long life stories.

"So, what's up with your mom?"

"What do you mean?"

"I could hear that Estelle woman's message on your phone. Why do you keep the volume so loud? You're going to go deaf. Anyway, I could hear her saying your mom couldn't stay there and you know why."

Ugh. Now she had to 'fess up.

"My mother is a hoarder."

"Like on those TV shows?"

"Worse probably."

"Huh."

"Huh?" she said.

"What?"

"That's all you have to say? Don't you want to make fun of me or judge me?"

"Why would I do that?"

"Because my mom is a freaking hoarder!" she said.

"Kelly, that has nothing to do with you. Is that why you didn't want me to take you to Atlanta?"

"Partially," she admitted. "I've been judged my whole life because of my parents. I worked hard to build the life I have in Whiskey Ridge. No one knew me there when I came to town, and I liked it. I could be who I was."

"And who is that?"

"I don't know anymore," she said softly before she leaned her head back, closed her eyes and enjoyed the silence.

CHAPTER 8

*W*hen she opened her eyes again, the lights of Atlanta were on the horizon. Quinn had turned the radio on at a low volume and was listening to contemporary country. She wasn't a fan of country normally, but something about it felt soothing right now.

"Have a nice nap?" he asked with a chuckle.

"Sorry. I guess class wore me out," she said, adjusting her hair and nonchalantly touching the corner of her mouth to check for drool. No drool.

"I think you're suffering from mental exhaustion, Kelly," he said.

"Maybe." She told him to get off at the next exit as they made it to the edge of the city. "Turn right up here just after the gas station."

They pulled into the hospital parking lot a few moments later. Kelly tried to gather herself, but she had a hard time. Normally, she saw her mother and got to go home. This time her mother would be coming with her, and that thought scared her to death.

"Ready?" Quinn asked softly, obviously picking up on her anxiety. She nodded and opened her door before he had a chance to make it around the other side of the truck.

An older woman sat at the front desk of the ER.

"Can I help you?"

"Yes, ma'am. My mother is here in the ER. Her house burned… Edie Cole is her name," Kelly said as the woman typed something into the computer.

"I'll buzz the door. She's in room eight," the woman said, pointing to two large double doors to her left. Kelly looked at Quinn.

"You want me to stay out here?" he asked. She knew she should say yes, but for some reason she couldn't. She was tired of dealing with major life events alone.

"No. Come with me. If you don't mind, that is." She stared up into his beautiful hazel eyes and felt her legs start to go weak again. Maybe he was right - she was exhausted.

"I don't mind at all. Let's go," he said, putting his hand on the small of her back as he guided her toward the door. Something about the way he led her made her feel safe for the first time in her life.

They walked down the corridor, and Kelly was

unable to keep herself from glancing into the rooms as she passed. Sick people, kids with broken arms, a man doubled over with abdominal pain… And then, room eight. Door closed. Her mother inside. She stopped.

"I don't know if I can do this," she said softly, turning away from the door.

"You can do this, Kelly." He grabbed her shoulders and turned her around to face him. "Everything will be alright."

And she believed him. She had no reason to, but she did. He reached for the door and opened it to reveal Edie sitting on the side of the bed, arms crossed and obviously ready to leave.

"Well, for Christ's sake, it's about time you showed up!" her mother chided as she stood up and grabbed her purse from the chair next to the bed. "Who the hell is this?"

Quinn chuckled. "Mother, honestly! Stop being so rude. This is my friend, Quinn, and he drove me here because my car broke down."

"Did you let it run out of gas again, Kelly? Remember when you did that in high school and Mr. Evans had to drive all the way…"

"Mother! Stop! Can we stop talking about random crap and get to the point? Your house burned to the ground because of all of your precious belongings!" Edie's face went white.

"To the ground?" Oh no… Kelly had no idea that

her mother didn't know the whole story yet. She felt horrible about blurting it out like that, but maybe her mother needed a reality check.

"Yes, Mom. To the ground. It's a total loss," Kelly said quietly as she sat down in the chair across from her mother. Edie slid back down onto the bed.

"What am I going to do?"

"I don't know just yet, but I do know you'll have to come home with me for awhile. I came… actually we came… to get you."

"I can't go home with you. We'll kill each other!" Edie said.

"Mom, neither one of us has a choice tonight. Tomorrow, we'll start making some plans, but for now we need to go. I'm springing you out of this joint," Kelly said, summoning a small smile and reaching out for her mother's hand.

Edie smiled back, giving Kelly a glimpse of the mother she'd always wished she had. "Then let's go."

After signing more forms, they loaded up in the truck and started toward the interstate when Edie suddenly piped up.

"Take me to my house," she demanded.

"Mom, it's late and…"

"I don't give a crap what time it is! I need to see it for myself!"

Kelly looked pleadingly at Quinn knowing he must've been exhausted after teaching classes all night and then driving hours in the dark. "Do you mind?"

"I don't mind at all, Kelly," he said with a smile as he reached out and stroked her hand for a brief moment. It sent chills up her spine.

She gave him directions to the house which was just a few blocks away. When they pulled up, one of the fire trucks was still on the scene, cleaning up the area of the street where they'd been parked. The three of them got out of the car and stood beside the fire truck.

"Can I help you?" a young fireman asked.

"No. Thank you. This is my mother's house," Kelly said. Edie stood beside her, staring at the house with her mouth hanging open. It was definitely a total loss.

"My God…" was all Edie managed to breathe out.

"I'm sorry for your loss, ma'am," the fireman said before he went back to work.

And then they drove toward Whiskey Ridge, and Kelly wondered how many more times her life would change in the blink of an eye.

* * *

THE DRIVE WAS FAIRLY quiet as Edie fell asleep in the back seat of the large pickup truck. When she suddenly woke up about thirty minutes from home, it was to announce her inability to wait to go to the bathroom. It was after midnight, but Quinn stopped at the nearest gas station he could find.

"I'll be a little while. I ate tacos for dinner... before my house burned down," she announced as she got out of the truck and headed into the convenience store.

Kelly covered her eyes and shook her head in embarrassment. Quinn laughed.

"I'm so sorry. I don't know why she feels the need to announce her digestive issues in such detail," Kelly said.

"It's okay. I find it pretty humorous, actually. She definitely doesn't have a filter between her mouth and brain, huh?"

"Never has. I think the drugs did something to her because my grandma said she was pretty normal until then."

"Drugs?"

"Oh yeah. Lots and lots of them. Her and my father."

"You're an amazing woman, Kelly Cole," he said with a smile. She finally looked at him.

"Why do you say that?"

"Look at what you've accomplished and how you've turned out even though you were raised in that environment. Amazing."

"Well, I don't feel so amazing these days," she said, leaning her head against the back of her seat.

"We all go through rough times, but you'll make it. And you'll be better for it," he said.

"How are you so sure?"

"Because I've done it. I thought I would die when Penny died. I thought I would never be able to get out of bed again. Never smile or laugh again. I felt so guilty the first time I wanted to laugh at a TV show, but then I realized she wouldn't want that for me. She would want me to go on, so I did. And you will too. Whatever has you so anxious inside... so sad... you'll come through it."

Before she could respond, her mother reappeared, banging on the window for Kelly to unlock the door. Quinn chuckled again and they were on their way home.

* * *

As they entered the city limits of Whiskey Ridge, Kelly could feel her stomach tighten into a knot. Her mother was coming home with her. She had nothing. No clothes, no possessions, for the first time in many years. But given the chance, she would accumulate more stuff as fast as she could.

"Where to?" Quinn asked.

"Oh, turn left at the stop sign. Then right onto Sycamore. My driveway is the second one on the right," she said, pointing toward her house in the dark hours of the early morning. By the time she would get her mother settled in, the sun would be coming up.

"You mean down here?" Quinn asked as he slowly turned down the first road.

"Yes…" she said, wondering why he was double checking with her when she'd just said it thirty seconds ago. Maybe he wasn't listening because he had to be tired. Poor guy.

"Just checking," he muttered. She glanced in his direction, and he suddenly seemed tense but she didn't know why. There was no smile, no relaxed look on his face.

"Are you okay?" she whispered, not wanting her loud mother to jump into the conversation.

"What?"

"You look tense."

"Nah. Just very tired," he said, the smile appearing back on his lips. But it looked forced, and there was almost a painful look in his eyes. She was too tired to think much of it tonight, but maybe she would ask him tomorrow.

Tomorrow. It was already tomorrow. What would she do about work? And her car? Ugh.

"Right here," she said, pointing as he drove closer to her driveway. She heard what she thought was his breath catch in his throat, but then her mother piped up out of nowhere.

"Holy crap! We're out in the boondocks, Kelly! Why on God's green earth would you want to live way out here?"

"Honestly, mother... Do you ever stop?" she groaned, rolling her eyes as Quinn slowly pulled down her driveway. Even in the dark, he seemed to be gripping the steering wheel with all his might. Maybe he had to poop.

Quinn stopped the truck and turned it off as Kelly got out with her keys in hand. He opened the door for Edie and helped her down out of the vehicle.

"Why is this blessed thing so freaking tall?" Edie complained as her feet touched down on the driveway.

"Closer to God," Quinn said with a half hearted chuckle. Edie didn't smile and walked toward the front door.

"I need to hit the bathroom again. Where is it?" she asked before Kelly had even opened the door. Once she did key the lock, Edie pushed past her and headed into the house.

"On the left, mother," Kelly called as she turned around to face Quinn. She closed the front door and looked at him wearily. "Listen, thank you so much..."

Quinn waved his hand in front of his face. "No problem. Really. I enjoy long night-time drives to the city," he said, a hint of a smile coming back to his face.

"And older female hoarders with irritable bladders?" Kelly asked.

"Love them especially," he said. "So, can I ask you something?"

"I suppose…"

"Does this mean we can call a truce now? Maybe actually be friends?" He gasped and put his hand over his mouth as if he was in shock. Kelly chucked him in the arm.

"Fine. I guess you're not so terribly bad," she said, smiling a little more than she'd imagined was possible during the wee hours of the morning. Part of her would rather stand on the porch all night, flirting with Quinn Maverick, instead of dealing with her crazy mother in her house.

"Well, goodnight, Kelly," Quinn said, backing up toward his truck.

"Goodnight," she said, closing her door and wishing she could leave with him.

"Who's he?" Edie asked as soon as Kelly closed the door. She could see his headlights slowly backing out of her driveway through the living room window. She closed her eyes and drew a deep breath before turning to face her mother.

"He's a friend," she said, thankful to have such a simple explanation.

"Yeah, sure. And I'm Aretha Franklin," her mother said, as she'd done a million times in her life.

"You're couldn't hold a tune in a bucket, and you're as pale as a ghost, mother, so you're no Aretha," Kelly said as she walked toward the kitchen for a glass of water. She wanted something stronger, but getting drunk at 1am wasn't the best idea for a grown woman.

"You know, you could be a little nicer. My house did burn down tonight. I barely made it out alive!" her mother said. Kelly started to shake as she turned around.

"Seriously? You want me to feel what? Sorry for you?"

"Well, any normal person certainly would!"

"Mom, you brought this on yourself! That house was a fire hazard and had been for years. I just told you this when I visited, for goodness sakes! It's hard to feel sorry for someone who wouldn't listen!"

Edie jutted her chin out and made a grunting sound, her typical response when she had no comeback. Kelly felt guilt starting to creep into her body. She walked toward her mother and put her hand on Edie's arm.

"Look, Mom, I'm so grateful you got out of there alive, but I'm exhausted and mentally drained. Let's get some sleep and tomorrow we'll figure out a place for you to live..." she said as she started walking toward the bedrooms.

"Excuse me?" Edie whipped around and grabbed her daughter's arm. "I thought I was staying here."

"Let's talk about this tomorrow," Kelly repeated

but Edie didn't budge. She had that look in her eyes that Kelly had seen so many times growing up. Anger. Resentment. Stubbornness.

"We'll talk about this right now, young lady." Kelly sighed.

"Fine, mother, have it your way. You cannot stay here long term. This is my home. My sanctuary. And it's clean and tidy and comfortable."

"It feels like a museum."

"Maybe so, but it's my oasis, and I'm sorry... but you won't ruin that for me. It took me years..."

"Wah, wah, wah... I've heard this story a million times. Your terrible childhood. Your awful parents. You're an adult now, Kelly. Get over it!"

Kelly's blood felt like it was literally boiling in her veins. Her mother would never understand because she couldn't. Her brain was fried from the drugs she did for years. Her viewpoint on the world was just "different" and that couldn't be undone.

"You can take the room on the right," Kelly said without engaging her mother. "There are fresh linens on the bed. Good night, mother."

With that, she walked down the hall into her own room and shut the door.

CHAPTER 9

When Kelly woke up a few hours later, she smelled coffee and bacon. Had she been sleepwalking? Maybe she was at a four star hotel and cabana boys would appear in her room at any minute...

"Wake up!" her mother yelled from the doorway after swinging the door open.

Kelly groaned and rolled over to look at the clock. It was only seven. A whopping four hours of sleep had just not been enough. She called Maggie and asked her to open the spa and then padded into the kitchen where her mother stood wearing one of her robes. Her nice, plush $150 robe from New York City. Her splurge from two years ago. And now it had a coffee stain on it. Just great.

Edie stood in front of the stove, bacon grease popping up and drenching the microwave above it.

Flour was all over the counters and there was another big coffee spill right next to the pot that she hadn't bothered to clean up.

"This place is a wreck! How did you already make such a big mess?" Kelly asked as she started frantically wiping the coffee spill.

"Oh, good Lord. What's a little mess? I'm cooking for goodness sakes!" Edie said, yelling over the loud exhaust fan as she tried to suck the smoke out of the kitchen.

"Maybe you could clean as you go..." Kelly continued as she focused on cleaning up after her mother. She raked the flour into her hand and tossed it into the sink.

"Well, maybe you could be more grateful that someone is cooking a nice breakfast for you," Edie said, glaring at her daughter. "These are your grandma's homemade biscuits."

"You remember the recipe?"

"Of course I do! I love to cook. I just haven't had a reason to in a long time," Edie said continuing her process.

"You mean you didn't have space to," Kelly mumbled. She didn't remember her mother being a good cook, but then again she was the one who had to do most of the cooking for the household anyway. Her sister certainly didn't do anything.

Edie finished up and walked to the table with a

plate of biscuits, some overcooked bacon and a pitcher of orange juice.

"Eat up," she said as she turned to get two glasses from the cabinet.

"I don't really eat breakfast…"

"Eat," Edie said again. "Probably why you don't have a boyfriend. You're way too skinny."

"Thanks," Kelly said, rolling her eyes. She took a bite of the almost black bacon and started to gag.

"Jelly?" Edie asked as she looked through the refrigerator.

"I don't eat processed sugar, so I don't own jelly."

"Good God, what is going on with you?" Edie asked.

"Sugar is poison."

"No, sugar is dang good on biscuits… in the form of jelly."

"I'll make note of that."

"I'll go to the grocery store today and get us some real food," Edie said as she shoveled a piece of bacon into her mouth. Kelly took a bite of her grandmother's biscuits and was pretty sure she was rolling over in her grave. They tasted like sheetrock, and Kelly would probably choose to eat sheetrock with a little jelly before she'd take another bite of those biscuits.

"Listen, I'm running late for work. I need to go get a shower and wake up." Kelly started toward the hallway when she noticed a truck sitting at the top of her driveway. It was Quinn's truck. She opened the door and walked outside just as he got out of his driver's side door.

"Hey!" she called from the front porch. He seemed startled when she called out to him, and she wasn't sure why didn't pull down closer to the house.

"Good morning. Nice outfit," he said as he walked closer to the house. Kelly looked down and remembered that she was wearing her pink kitty cat pajama set and looked more like a ten year old girl than a grown woman.

"Thanks. I was a little tired and didn't really care who I am impressed with my PJ attire at two in the morning," she said with a smile. "Why'd you park way up there?"

Quinn turned and looked at his truck. "Just didn't want to startle you by coming close to the house so early in the morning."

"I don't typically shoot people just because they pull into my driveway, Quinn."

"Noted."

"What are you doing here anyway?"

"I… uh… your mom left something in my truck." He seemed to be stumbling over his words.

"What'd she leave?"

"This," he said, pulling a small hair clip out of his pocket. Kelly laughed as she took it from his hand. "Why are you laughing?"

"Well, first I'm laughing because you came all the

way over here to give me a cheap little hair clip at seven in the morning. And secondly, I'm laughing because this was my hair clip in elementary school. I can't believe my mother somehow managed to keep up with it after all these years."

"I thought it might be special, so I wanted to return it," he said, a little bit of irritation in his voice.

"Don't get all offended. I was just surprised to see you here so early." She thought they'd formed a friendship, but he really did seem to be upset about something. "Are you okay?"

"Sure. Why wouldn't I be?" he asked, looking down at his shoes for a moment before making eye contact.

"I don't know. You just seem… distracted," she said.

"I'm tired, Kelly."

"Of course. I'm so sorry. Thank you again…"

"Please stop thanking me. Listen, I have to go, but I'll see you around, okay?" he said as he turned and headed back up the driveway.

She would never understand men.

* * *

"So your mom is at your house right now?" Maggie asked, chomping on her strong smelling watermelon gum. Kelly hated the stuff, but Maggie insisted on chewing it constantly.

"Yep," Kelly said, feeling her teeth grinding together as she typed something onto her spreadsheet.

"And you're okay with that?" Maggie asked as she leaned against the desk and twirled one of Kelly's prized red pens around with her finger. Kelly slapped her hand on it to stop the spinning.

"No. I'm most definitely not okay with it but what can I do? She has no place to go." She leaned back in her chair and sighed. "She's going to turn my house into a garbage dump."

"Mel, you're a grown woman. You can handle this. Is she rebuilding her house?"

"Nope. She has decided to stay in Whiskey Ridge until she gets her insurance money and then travel around the world, starting with Vegas."

Maggie's mouth dropped open. "Is that even legal?"

"Don't get me started. All I know is that she's currently sitting in her bathrobe on my very expensive sofa, probably watching court TV shows and eating my stash of dark chocolate." Kelly plopped her forehead onto the desk in front of her. "She's going to give me a stroke. I just know it."

"You've got to calm down, girlfriend. Seriously. I think you're being a bit over-dramatic. Don't you?"

"I wish I was…"

"Hey, ladies," Quinn said from the doorway. Maggie's mouth dropped open again. Never one for subtleness, Maggie wore every one of her emotions on her sleeve. And her face.

"Hey, Quinn… Nice to see you," she gushed. Kelly wanted to throw up.

"Nice dress, Maggie," he said with his best Hollywood smile. Kelly reminded herself that he was her friend now and she couldn't secretly loathe him. He'd been there in her time of need, and she was going to try to be his friend and stop lusting after him.

"Thanks," she said, turning about the same shade of red as her hair. It was like she'd been transformed into an eight year old girl, flirting with her schoolyard crush across the playground.

"Mind if I talk to Kelly alone for a minute?"

"Oh, sure," Maggie said, giving Kelly a knowing glance as she grabbed a folder and went into the foyer to welcome a new client.

Quinn walked around to the front of Kelly's desk and sat down in the plush tan chair. "How's it going?"

"Oh, just dandy," she said with a fake smile. "Things are perfect. I have a sixty year old woman currently staining my couch with *my* expensive dark chocolate while watching Judge Judy, and I'm sitting here having inner panic attacks every few minutes. I feel like I just won the lottery!"

Quinn started laughing which only served to irritate her further. Assessing the look on her face, he stopped himself and bit his lip.

"I'm sorry. I know it's not funny, but seeing you like this kind of tickles my funny bone."

"Great. Thanks. I thought we were friends," she grumbled as she closed her laptop and looked at him.

"You're right. We are friends, and that's why I'm here right now."

"I'm waiting..." she said, tapping her fingers on her desk.

"Well, I thought maybe you'd like a night out." Her stomach started to turn upside down.

"Are you asking me on a date, Quinn Maverick?" The hope in her own voice almost made her cringe.

"Um, no..." he stammered. "We're friends, right? Can't friends go out for dinner?"

Suddenly, she felt completely let down and she didn't want to admit to herself why. Of course he didn't want to date her. Why would he? They were nothing alike, and she was a stick in the mud compared to him.

"Sure. Just wanted to clarify so you didn't get the wrong impression," she said, trying desperately to save herself from an embarrassing situation.

"Great. I'll pick you up at seven," he said authoritatively as he stood up and walked toward the door.

"Wait a minute! You mean tonight?"

"Well, yeah..."

"I can't go tonight. My house is probably already a disaster area with the queen of hoarding having full control all day."

"Fine. Then I'll come to your house. We can have a nice family dinner with your mom. Maybe she can tell us more about her digestive system."

"You're not funny. How is that taking me for a night out?"

"Exactly. I'll see you at seven. And dress a little bit fancy." With that, he walked out and Kelly was left wondering what this was really all about.

* * *

WHEN SHE ARRIVED home after working a long day with no lunch break, Kelly was exhausted. The last thing she wanted to do was face her mother, or her house for that matter, but she knew there was no way around it. She couldn't just abandon her home and run away, although she'd thought about it a few times throughout the day.

She thought about it when her mother called at eleven to yell at her about the remote control not working. Kelly had pointed her to the battery drawer. Yes, she had a battery drawer. It was nice and neat and made sense for her life. And when somebody needed batteries, who did they call? Actually, they probably just went and bought batteries. Truth be told, nobody called her for batteries. But it still made her feel better to be prepared.

She also thought about running away when her mom called at 1:30 to complain that the mailman came to the door and delivered a package. And then at 2:30 when she called to complain that she was hungry and Kelly only had healthy food in the house.

As she keyed the door, she prepared for the worst but was shocked to find very little out of place. In fact, it almost looked like her mother had wiped down the kitchen counters. How could that be?

"Mom?" she called out. Edie came out from her bedroom wearing a pair of Kelly's shorts and a T-shirt. "I see you helped yourself to my clothing."

"Well, would you rather I prance around naked? I'm sure all of Whiskey Ridge would be talking within the hour. How many people live in this town anyway? Like fifty or sixty?" Her mother's smart remarks about the size of her town were starting to grate on her nerves.

"About ten thousand, actually."

"Ooohhh…. Thriving metropolis you have here."

"Mother, honestly. Do you have to be contrary about everything?"

"Contrary? Who uses that word?"

"I do!" Kelly yelled. "And I have healthy food and a battery drawer. And a nice mailman named Sam who brings me my packages because I bake him homemade oatmeal raisin cookies at Christmas and give his wife an occasional free facial. This is my life, mother. And I love it!"

"Do you?" her mother asked in a accusing tone. "Or are you just trying to be everything I wasn't?"

Kelly snarled at her mother. "Can you blame me?" There was so much more she could say, and even wanted to say, but what good would it do? She couldn't undo the past and yelling at her mother only attracted more negative energy into her life. And if there was one thing that running a spa had taught her, it was the importance of controlling the energy around her.

"You can never let it go. And you'll be miserable your whole life. Everything has to be just the perfect way. For goodness sakes, you had to send a freaking maid to clean the house today? You couldn't trust me for one day here alone?"

"What? You let someone in here to clean?"

"Yeah. Her name was Gertrude. She was a rotund woman with wiry red hair, but she seemed to do a good job. Said she'd already been paid. Are you saying you didn't hire her?"

"No, I didn't hire anyone. I clean my house myself," Kelly said confused. She walked into the kitchen and saw that it was spotless, as was the living room and bathroom. The only room where things were starting to get messy was her mother's room, of course.

The thought of this random woman in her house

made her nervous and very uncomfortable. Was she some kind of strange criminal, going around Whiskey Ridge cleaning houses and staking out the joint looking for diamonds? Maybe she'd been watching too much Dateline NBC. And since she didn't have any diamonds, she couldn't figure out any reason why this woman would've been in her house.

"Did she leave a business card? What was she driving?"

"No and I don't know. I was watching TV in my tiny little bedroom. You really need more space. This house is…"

"Mother! You had like four feet of usable space in your house and…"

Suddenly, the doorbell rang interrupting her thoughts and startling her.

"Maybe it's the cleaning lady coming back to kill us," her mother said, laughing at her own joke as she walked into the kitchen. Kelly rolled her eyes and opened the door to find Quinn standing there, dressed in a dark pair of jeans and a pressed gray button up shirt, looking like the best thing she'd ever seen in her life.

And she wasn't ready. And it was seven on the dot.

"Good evening," he said with a smile. "Weren't you wearing that today?"

"Very observant, Mr. Maverick," she said,

opening the door and inviting him inside. Edie peeked her head around the kitchen door, rolled her eyes and disappeared from sight again.

"She doesn't like me," he whispered. "And I'm starting to wonder if you do."

She smiled, realizing she wasn't being very hospitable. "Sorry. I just found out some random stranger came here today and cleaned my house."

"Isn't that a good thing? I mean you were worried about your mother destroying the place, right?"

"Good that it's clean, but bad that I don't know the woman."

"Gertrude is a trustworthy lady. Now, get ready so we can make our reservations at Limelight."

"Wait. How did you know her name?"

"Friends help friends, especially when they're stressed out. I knew what your mother would do to this house, so I helped out," he said softly so Edie couldn't hear.

Kelly's heart suddenly melted into a puddle of goo on the floor. She'd never known a man like Quinn Maverick.

"You did this?" she asked as she moved closer so she was about a foot away from him.

"No big deal. Really. She cleans my place on Tuesdays."

"Quinn, I..."

"Are we going to eat dinner or what?" Edie called

from the kitchen. "I mean, who comes for a visit at the dinner hour?" Quinn chuckled under his breath.

"Mother! Have some manners!" Kelly called back. "I'm so sorry..." she whispered.

"Don't worry, Edie. I've got a pizza on its way for you to enjoy tonight," he called out to her. Edie popped her head back around the corner and gave him a quizzical look. "I'm taking your daughter out for some much needed relaxation time."

"What toppings?" Edie asked without acknowledging what he'd said.

"Well, I had to guess, but I chose sausage and green peppers." Kelly thought that was an odd choice. Why not choose pepperoni or plain cheese? She liked plain cheese herself. No muss, no fuss.

Edie grunted in approval and went back into the kitchen. "How did you know she'd like sausage and green peppers, of all things?" she asked with a giggle.

"Well, I think she's got kind of a spicy personality, so they seemed obvious." He winked at her and she felt the heat start to rise throughout her body, threatening to send flushed redness to her face.

"I'd better get dressed," she said as she quickly turned and made her way to her bedroom. This was going to be one interesting night, that much was sure.

CHAPTER 10

*A*fter quickly getting dressed and touching up her minimal makeup, Kelly was ready to go. They said a fast goodbye to Edie, who was already chowing down on her pizza by the time Kelly was ready, and climbed into Quinn's waiting truck.

He was a man's man, with a truck big enough to crush a few other trucks. Southern to the core and a black belt, he would seem to most outsiders to be tough, rugged and impossible to penetrate, but Kelly caught glimpses of a softer side. A funny guy with a sharp wit and the occasional bit of sarcasm, Quinn was a mix of everything most women wanted.

But she sensed he had some secrets of his own, perhaps even bigger secrets than she'd been keeping about her upbringing.

Talk in the truck had mostly been centered around work, his history of learning karate and her relationship with Maggie. Being that Whiskey Ridge was a small dot of a town, they were at Limelight, the only fancy restaurant in town, in five minutes flat.

Quinn walked around and opened the passenger door to help her down, and she second guessed her choice of attire. Wearing her favorite short red dress and strappy black heels, it had been hard enough to climb up into the truck, much less climb down without mooning half the town. Thank God she was wearing her expensive panties, although she wasn't sure why.

He took her hand and whisked her down without any apparent effort at all. When her feet hit the ground, he let her go and smiled.

"What?"

"I didn't want to say so in front of your mother, but holy crap you look hot in that dress," he said, his rough voice cracking a bit.

"Thank you... *friend*," she said, with special emphasis on "friend".

"Would Maggie tell you that you look hot?"

"Well, yes…"

"Then don't be sarcastic….*friend*," he said with a wink before putting his hand on her lower back and guiding her toward the door. She had to admit, just the simple act of feeling a man's hand on her back, guiding her, was a welcome respite from her recent independence.

When they sat down at their table overlooking a small lake, Kelly felt she could finally take a deep breath after days of anxiety dealing with her mother. The smell of steaks cooking on the grill was over-taking her senses, and she realized she had missed lunch and was starving.

"This place is beautiful. I've never been here before," she said looking around at the elegant decor.

"Seriously? You've lived here a lot longer than I have. Why haven't you been here?" Quinn asked.

"No one ever brought me," she said as she hungrily reached for a piece of the bread that the waiter had brought to the table. Since this wasn't a date, she was going to freely eat like a pig instead of nibble on salad as she would normally be tempted to do.

"Wait, didn't you have a longterm boyfriend?"

"How'd you know that?" she asked.

"Maggie likes to talk," he said with a laugh. And that was an understatement. Maggie, God love her, couldn't keep her big trap shut. Plus, she'd been trying to push Quinn on Kelly, both literally and figuratively, since he'd shown up in town.

"Big mouth," Kelly muttered. "Yes, I dated Rio for a year..."

"Rio?" he said, almost doing a spit-take with his water.

"Um, you have no room to talk, Quinn Maverick. Where did you get a name like that anyway?"

"What can I say? My mom knew how cool I would be one day."

"Good Lord…" she said with a smile as she took another bite of her bread. Carbs had never been her friend, but right now she was so hungry she could've eaten the back of a Volkswagen bug.

"But back to you. Why didn't Rio ever bring you here?"

"Rio was… how do I say this… different." Yeah, that was an understatement.

"Different how?"

"Artsy. Flaky. Lazy." She wanted to add other words like "cheater", "dirt bag" and "guy-who-is-going-straight-to-hell-for-cheating-on-me", but she refrained.

"Wow, sounds like quite a catch," he said with a laugh. "And you were with him because…"

Kelly stopped for a moment and looked at him. "I have no idea."

They both broke into laughter. It was true. She had no idea why she chose Rio in the first place. He certainly wasn't her type at all, but she didn't really know who her type was anyway.

A part of her had secretly hoped that Quinn Maverick was her type, but he obviously wasn't interested since he kept emphasizing the fact that they were friends and friends only. And she wasn't altogether sure that she wanted to be with another man anytime soon. Her life was in upheaval at the present time, and the last thing she needed was to add a relationship to the mix.

"So you dated an artsy, fartsy guy for a whole year and you don't know why?"

"Pretty much. I mean he was Brazilian and cooked the most amazing food, but that's hardly a reason to stay with someone so long, I suppose."

"And what happened to him?"

"Oh, he slept with my best friend of six years, in my bed, and then whisked her off to live a lifestyle of laziness in Hawaii with him," she said, popping the last piece of her bread in her mouth and then smiling with a look of achievement on her face as if to say "top that one".

"Lovely. Great friend you had there."

"Tell me about it."

"So, I have another question."

"Okay…"

"Where's your father?" he asked softly.

"What are you, a reporter?" She especially hated talking about her father. It was a lot easier to talk about her mother because she at least interacted with her, but talking about not having a father in her life – and being abandoned by him – was a lot more difficult.

"Sorry, is that too private?"

"Yes, but I'll tell you anyway," she said with a half-hearted smile.

"You don't have to, Kelly," he replied, taking a sip of his water.

She knew she didn't have to, but for some reason she didn't mind opening up to Quinn. It felt comfortable and safe. "My father is in prison."

Quinn couldn't help but have a look of shock on his face. "Oh. Wow…"

"Haven't seen him in years and don't plan to. His drug habit led to some other poor choices, and I just don't need that negativity in my life. Plus, he was never a real father to me anyway." She tried to sound unattached, but the truth was it did hurt. Growing up without a father hadn't been easy. Knowing she would never have a father to walk her down the aisle one day was upsetting, but more so because she didn't know if she would ever get to walk down an aisle as the actual bride.

"I'm so sorry you grew up in that environment, Kelly. But you definitely rose above it, and it's made you stronger."

"Maybe," she said, "but it's also made me 'tightly wound', according to just about everybody I know." She wanted to say "including you", but held her tongue. But she knew he was thinking it because he had said as much as soon as they met.

"I'm sorry I judged you so harshly when we met. I understand why you protect yourself and your space now. I really mean it," he said softly. Her stomach did a flip flop.

"It's okay. And I'm sorry I misjudged you too," she said. "But when you called me a chick, I almost body slammed you."

Before he could respond, the waiter came to take their order.

Kelly enjoyed a nice juicy steak and a side salad, which was more food than she would normally consume but she was having such a good time talking and laughing with Quinn that she felt lighter and less anxious than she had in years. Or maybe ever.

He was the most easygoing guy she'd ever known, telling her about his years growing up in Tennessee with a stay at home mother and a father who was a traveling salesman. Honestly, his upbringing sounded like Leave It To Beaver, and she envied what he'd experienced as a child.

Lots of love. Huge family. Even a real white picket fence.

"So," she said, between bites of her salad, "do your parents still live in Tennessee?"

"My mom does. My father passed away three years ago. Brain cancer," he said, sorrow landing on his face. Her heart hurt for him.

"I'm so sorry, Quinn. He sounds like he was a wonderful father."

"He was, and I'm eternally grateful for all he

taught me. One day, I hope to be half the father he was."

The thought of Quinn Maverick as someone's father made Kelly almost feel jealous for the child. What she would've given for a man like him to have raised her. Maybe one day she'd have a husband like him to help raise her children. At least she hoped so.

"Can I ask you something?" he said as the waiter started to clear the table to make way for their dessert.

"Yes, Mr. Inquisitive. Would you like to know my blood type or shoe size?" she said with a giggle.

"Neither. But I would guess a size seven on the shoe size." How did he know that? "Anyway, I was wondering about that cross at the edge of your property. Looks like some kind of memorial?"

"Oh, yes. There was a terrible car accident there a little over a year ago."

"Did you see it?"

"No, but I heard it. I was home from work. The noise was horrific. It was a very violent crash." Thinking about it made her cringe, and she really didn't want to talk about it, especially when they were having such a lovely time.

"Do you know who it was?" he asked. She realized he wasn't letting it go, so she might as well tell the whole story so they could move on to happier topics.

"No. It was a woman. She seemed to have taken

115

the curve too fast. I ran to see if I could help, but the car caught fire and... well, there was nothing I could do."

"Did you see her?" he asked softly, leaning over the table.

"Briefly. She was passed out. I think she hit her head. I tried to open the door, but that's when the car went up in flames... Sorry, I don't like to talk about it. I still have nightmares sometimes." She hated that knotted up feeling in her stomach. For weeks, she saw that poor woman in her dreams. Her head leaned back against the seat, apparently unconscious, which was probably a good thing in the end. Her sincere prayer was that the woman didn't feel anything.

"I understand. I'm sorry. I was just curious about it," he said. "Does anyone ever come visit it?"

"Occasionally. There's a guy I see out there sometimes, but he only started coming a few months after the accident."

"Have you talked to him?"

"No, I never wanted to intrude on his grief," she said, as the waiter put cheesecake in front of her. "This is a real downer, Quinn. Can we talk about something else?" she asked.

"Of course," he said, and they continued telling each other their life stories.

* * *

LIVING with her mother was becoming harder by the day. Even with Gertrude cleaning the house once a week, Edie could still make a mess as quick as a drunk six-year old. Of course, Kelly had never met a drunk six-year old and could only imagine their mess-making abilities.

Edie was spending her Social Security money on garage sales, and she certainly wasn't setting any money aside in case the insurance company didn't pay out on her claim. After all, the fire was probably her fault given the state of her home. The cause hadn't been determined yet, but Kelly expected that her mother would be devastated when the results came in.

Since her "not date" with Quinn, she hadn't seen him too much except at her self defense classes. He'd hired a second instructor to help with his ever-growing business, and Kelly had met him a couple of times.

She'd started settling into living with the extra noise, and Quinn had even explained the meanings of some of the Korean phrases he used in class. In other words, she was adjusting to her new way of life. Messy mother, loud sexy friend.

But something had been nagging at her for the last couple of weeks, and it was something unexpected. Her sister. She'd started receiving emails from her, evidently from France, just after her date with Quinn.

First, they were "hey, just touching base" sorts of emails, which was strange all by itself since Vivienne never "checked in" with her family. Maybe once a year on Christmas, they'd get a fancy gold foil card all the way from Paris. Edie would brag on her "successful" daughter and Kelly would seethe with rage silently.

But these emails had a different tone. A "testing the waters" kind of tone that made no sense to Kelly. Her sister was living the high life with her rich husband in the most romantic place on Earth. Why was she suddenly in contact?

Just out of sheer morbid curiosity, Kelly had continued responding and finally told Vivienne about their mother's current situation. Vivienne seemed to be somewhat concerned, almost like a normal daughter would respond, but then her snooty personality would come rearing its ugly head a few sentences later.

The fancy wine she drank.

The amazing places she visited.

The nice house she had.

And when Kelly would look around at her small town life with no boyfriend and no prospects, and her insane mother who was destroying her house, she found herself wanting to pack up and run away just like she did as soon as she turned eighteen.

Only she could never seem to escape the madness that was her life.

"Lost in thought?" Quinn said after finding her sitting on the steps in front of their building. She normally would've gone home at this time of day for her break, but her mother was there and she just couldn't do it.

"Oh, hey. Sorry, I didn't see you there..." she said, breaking a stick in half that she'd been holding in her hands. Throwing the little shards of it onto the ground below, she stared out at her rose bushes.

"Yeah, I could see that," he said with a laugh. "When's your next appointment?"

"Six. Why?"

"Come on," he said, standing up and pulling on her arm.

"Where are we going?" she asked as he continued his efforts to pull her from the steps.

"You'll see," was all he said as she followed him to his truck. A few minutes later, they were traveling down a gravel drive just on the edge of town. It was a part of town that Kelly rarely visited, mainly because it was so rural and out of the way. Even though Whiskey Ridge wasn't a thriving metropolis, she did prefer to stay in town so she could do her shopping and at least see the occasional person.

"I think this is private property, Quinn. These redneck boys up here will shoot us." Quinn started laughing.

"I **am** this redneck boy," he said, stopping the truck in front of a beautiful log cabin set way back off the road next to a lake. Kelly looked at him quizzically. "Kelly, this is my house."

"Oh…." she said with her hand on her chest. "You scared me."

Quinn climbed out and opened her door, whisking her to the ground like he did the last time she was in his truck. They walked toward the back of his truck instead of toward the house.

"What are we doing here?"

"Well, we have a couple of hours to kill, so I thought we could go fishing." He pulled two rods and a tackle box from the back of his truck. Kelly stood there in shock.

"Fishing? In the middle of a work day?"

"Don't tell me you're one of those women who won't bait her own hook," he said, furrowing his eyebrows at her.

"Of course not! I was raised in the South!" she said, taking one of the rods from his hand and marching toward the lake. Of course, she was totally lying. She'd never been fishing a day in her life, and she certainly didn't have a father to teach her how to bait a hook. But she'd be danged if Quinn Maverick was going to find that out.

As they walked down toward the lake, she ran through her mind all of the ways in which this was probably going to be a catastrophe, but it didn't stop her from at least trying to pretend she knew what in the heck she was doing.

There was a small dock with built-in benches on it on the left side of the lake, furthest from the cabin. They walked onto it and put down all of the gear. She was wearing a pair of capri pants and flats today, thankfully. Otherwise, stiletto heels might have proved to be disastrous in this situation.

Fishing is a silent activity, so the two of them sat together for the first few minutes, quietly baiting their hooks. When it became obvious that Kelly had no clue what she was doing, Quinn silently scooted closer to her and baited her hook with a worm before tossing her line into the water and handing the rod back to her.

"You're not going to make fun of me?" she said softly as she bumped his shoulder.

"Nope."

"Why not?" she asked, daring to take a glance at him. He met her glance.

"Because that wouldn't make me a very nice guy, now would it?" Dang, his voice was gruff and manly. She didn't answer, but instead turned away before he saw any hint of her longing for him to kiss her, and she was pretty sure her cheeks were red.

"You have a beautiful place here," she said as quietly as possible so as not to scare away the fish.

"Thanks. I needed a place to start my life over, and this place just felt right."

"Tell me about your wife, Quinn," she found

herself blurting out without thinking. It felt invasive, but she waited and allowed the silence to linger.

"We met in high school. I was the jock."

"Of course," she said laughing. He shot her a glance and continued.

"She was a cheerleader. Most popular girl in our tiny high school. Then we went off to college. I got a little too wild, and we broke up for a year while I figured out how to behave myself."

"Bad boy…"

He laughed. "Yeah, I was definitely not acting at a high level of maturity back then. Anyway, we got back together in our senior year. She got a teaching degree, and I got a my business degree. We had big plans, but then her father got sick."

"What was wrong?"

"He had ALS, and it was aggressive. She wanted to move back home to our little town in Tennessee and help take care of him, so we did a quickie wedding at the courthouse and moved back to take care of her Dad."

"That was kind of you."

"I loved him like a father. He was a good man," he said, his voice cracking a bit as he stared out over the water. "Anyway, he lived thirteen months. Died at home one morning as peacefully as we could hope. Her mother was devastated. They'd been together since they were eleven years old."

"Wow. That's a long love story," Kelly said, wishing that she had the same kind of story to tell.

"Yeah. It was something we wanted to emulate, but that's not how things went, unfortunately." He looked pained, and she could understand why. He'd lost his high school sweetheart. She wanted to ask how, but that felt way too intrusive in the moment, so she just let him talk.

"Things started off good, but we soon realized that the time apart had changed us. She was different. I was different. Our relationship was different. That one year had allowed me to grow up and into the man I wanted to become. She wanted to travel the world, but I wanted a quiet home life. Her father's illness was a great distraction at the time, but once he was gone and her mother was settled into her new life, things started the crumble. We even spent a few months separated, but we kept trying to pull it back together, you know?"

"I can understand that. I mean, I've never been married myself, but a marriage is something worth saving."

"Yeah, and we were trying when she..."

"When she died?"

"Yes. It was unexpected to say the least. There's never enough time..." She could see the tears welling up in his eyes, but he continued. "We had discussed divorce for the first time the day before."

She didn't know what to say, but she could only

imagine the guilt he was now living with. "I'm so sorry, Quinn."

He took a deep breath. "Thanks. But I'm doing a lot better now. Moving on, enjoying my work again… meeting new friends," he said with a smile. Her heart started beating faster, and she tried to will it to slow down. "Hey, I think you've got a bite!"

She turned to see her line being tugged into the water, and something pretty big was on the other end. He put his hands over hers and jerked it quickly and then started reeling it in. When they finally reeled it in, he told her it was the biggest bass he'd seen caught in the lake since he'd lived there.

"See? I told you I could fish!" she exclaimed as she held the fishing line up with her catch on the other end. When the fish wiggled, she screamed and dropped it as Quinn struggled to get it off the line and tossed it back into the water.

"Yeah, you're a pro," he said with a sarcastic laugh as they started gathering their supplies.

CHAPTER 11

*K*elly stared out the window of Quinn's cabin and looked at the mountains off in the distance. Whiskey Ridge was in the mountains, but they also surrounded it, each looking as though it had been painted in an array of blue shades.

"This view is gorgeous," she said as Quinn handed her a glass of sweet tea.

"Yeah, it was the main reason I wanted the property. The Blue Ridge mountains are my favorite place on earth," he said. "So, how's it going with your mother?"

"Ugh. Did you have to ruin a perfectly nice moment?" she said as she sat down on a bar stool in the breakfast area.

"Sorry."

"She seems happy, but I'm going nuts. And now my sister has started contacting me."

"The one in France?"

"Yep."

"That seems odd."

"I think so too. I'm not sure yet what her angle is, but I know there is one."

"Maybe she just misses you and your mother."

"Doubtful. Vicki… I'm sorry… Vivienne always has an agenda. She's a lot like our mother, which is why they didn't always get along. Do you have siblings?"

"I have two brothers. One lives overseas in Japan. He's a Marine. The other one lives in Texas with his wife and six kids."

"Six kids?" she said, almost spitting out her tea.

"Yep. They have all names that start with the letter 'I'," he said laughing.

"Wow, that would be hard to do. What are there names?"

"Isaiah, Isaac, Illiana, Ida, Ignacious and Igor." She could tell he was trying hard not to smile.

"You're pulling my leg, Quinn Maverick!" she said as she stood up and slapped at him. But, as was typical for Kelly, her foot got caught on the corner of the breakfast bar and she found herself falling forward toward the oven.

Yep. This was it. Total slow motion moment where her face was going to collide with the handle of the oven any second now. There'd be a black eye, maybe a broken nose, and Quinn would have a story to tell for years to come. She would be horribly disfigured and on pain medication which she would become addicted to and need one of those interventions…

But there was no pain. Instead, she found herself in his arms, staring at him face to face, their noses almost touching.

He'd caught her somehow.

"You okay?" he said, his voice lower and gruffer than she'd heard before, and she could've sworn that his breathing was more ragged. His hands were on both of her sides, holding her just below her armpits.

"Yeah… I'm fine…" she managed to breathe out, yet neither of them moved. It should've been awkward but it wasn't. They both stood there for what seemed like minutes, staring at each other and not speaking. Yet, it didn't seem like enough time at all either. "You saved me again," she finally said softly.

"Somebody has to take care of you." For some reason, those words felt like to antidote to every bad thing that had ever happened to her. No one had ever taken care of her. Not her mother. Certainly not her father. And Rio? Yeah, that one was laughable.

But it was exactly what Quinn Maverick had done since she'd met him. Saved her from a frisky date. Saved her when she needed a ride to Atlanta. Saved her house from her hoarding mother. And now saved her from a face plant.

She cleared her through and stepped back. "Thanks," she said, all too aware what was in his mind. He wanted to be friends, and she wasn't going to put herself out there to get rejected.

Kelly turned back toward the living room. "I can't believe you had me going about your brother..." she started to say as she looked out toward the mountains, but she felt Quinn's hand on her arm, turning her around to face him again.

She looked up into his green eyes and saw something she hadn't seen before. They were tender and soft, and she didn't know what to make of it. He said no words, but instead placed his hands first on her shoulders and then slid them up to her cheeks and just looked at her. And then slowly, amazingly, he leaned in, touching his lips against hers in what could only be described as the most sensuous kiss ever given on Earth.

For a moment, she stood there limp with her arms hanging by her sides like a puppet, but then she decided to make the most of the moment before he realized they were just friends. She slid her hands up his back, feeling the ripples of muscles under his shirt.

And then he pulled back.

"I'm sorry…" he said, stepping back a couple of feet. "I shouldn't have done that."

"It's… okay…." she stammered, unsure of what to say. It would've been pretty impossible to pretend she didn't enjoy it since she had been groping his muscular back just a few seconds before.

He ran his fingers through his hair and then she was sure she heard some kind of growl before he stepped forward and kissed her again. This time, there was more passion than sensuality and she almost lost her legs. Of course, she had no concerns that he wouldn't catch her.

And then again, he pulled back and made the same growling noise before he completely stepped away and started pacing. It was like watching a caged animal at the zoo, and she didn't know what to say or do. Finally, he spoke.

"This wasn't supposed to happen."

"Okay…"

"She's only been gone a year…" he said softly. And there it was. His late wife. He was feeling guilty for kissing another woman. That had to be it.

Kelly stepped toward him. He had a pained look on his face that she hadn't seen before, and she wanted to take it away but there was nothing she could do.

"Quinn…"

"I didn't want to like you. I mean, I wanted to be

friends. I thought I could say we were friends and it would just be true, you know? But it's not true."

"It's not?" she asked, the hopeful tone in her voice coming out whether she liked it or not. He looked at her and smiled.

"I just kissed you... twice."

"Yeah, I remember," she said with a smile.

"I just couldn't stop myself anymore."

"Anymore?"

"I've been struggling since the moment I met you, Kelly," he said, walking toward her. He stopped and put his hand on her cheek. "I can't stop thinking about you."

"Then don't," she said. And then she was late getting back to work.

* * *

MAGGIE SAT on the edge of Kelly's desk, her hand over her mouth in amazement, as Kelly leaned back in her chair with a look of sheer pleasure on her face.

"He kissed you? I can't believe it!" If it was possible, Maggie was even more excited than Kelly. Well, maybe not. Every part of her body still felt like it was lit up with electricity, and she had no idea how she would possibly concentrate on work for the rest of the day.

"Shhh…. He's going to hear you!" Kelly urged,

smacking her friend on the knee. "But, yes, he kissed me. A lot. And it was heaven."

"I thought you hated him?" Maggie said sarcastically.

"Shut up."

"So, tell me every little detail. Did ya'll…. You know….."

"No! Of course not! We just kissed, and honestly that was plenty for me. I've never been kissed that way in my life."

"That good, huh?"

"It made me want to write a sonnet. And I have no idea how to write a sonnet."

"Yeah, I've only been kissed good enough to write a haiku maybe," Maggie said dryly.

"I can't believe I've been missing that kind of passion in my life. Who knew?" It was true. She had never felt that way in her life. It was an all-consuming passion like she wanted to literally climb inside of Quinn's body and never leave. It was both exciting and terrifying at the same time, to be vulnerable and give up a part of herself.

"So do you think you'll start dating?" Maggie asked, pulling a piece of gum from her purse.

"I don't know. We didn't really talk about it. I know he's having a hard time moving on… after his wife…"

"Poor guy. It has to be hard."

"I'm just going to play it cool and see where things go."

"My, how life can change on a dime," Maggie said as she walked out to greet a customer.

* * *

SEVERAL DAYS HAD PASSED since their kissing scene, and Kelly hadn't seen Quinn's lips anywhere near hers. It was amazing how she already missed those lips, but maybe he'd made a decision not to pursue a relationship with her. Maybe the "friend thing" was all they would ever be.

Ugh. That thought made her sad and mad at herself for caring.

But the problem was that she did care. She cared a lot. How had she gone from thinking he was a jerk-face to wanting to kiss him for several hours a day?

"Hey!" she heard Quinn say as she was getting into her car to go home for her break.

"Hey yourself!" she said smiling. *Please kiss me. Please kiss me.*

Out of breath from running across the parking lot, Quinn stopped and caught his breath. Probably couldn't kiss while he was panting like that. She had to get her mind on something else.

"What's up?"

"Just haven't seen you much lately. My students

were in a testing cycle this week, so I've been really busy with that."

"Sure. I understand," she said.

"Heading home?"

"Yep. My mom called and said she needed me to come home. No idea what that's about."

"Maybe she got her insurance money and is moving out."

"From your lips to God's ears," she said, and then there it was again. Thoughts of his lips...

And how ironic it was that while she was thinking about his lips, he leaned in and planted a soft kiss on hers. Her legs started to go weak again, and she decided that adding a leg workout to her routine was something to look into for sure.

He pulled back and smiled at her. "Boy, I've missed that these last few days," he said with a smile. She felt like she could literally climb into his big green eyes and get lost for days.

"You have?"

"You haven't?"

"No comment," she said with a giggle and then climbed into her car. "See you later?"

"You can bet on it."

* * *

KELLY PULLED into the driveway of her home and wondered what her mother was up to inside. Maybe she had damaged something and wanted Kelly to see it in person. Maybe she was going to ask to move in permanently. Who knew with her mother.

After keying the lock, she opened the door to find her mother sitting on the sofa with her arms crossed. Although she had few belongings other than what Kelly had bought her for clothing, she had everything shoved into a plastic bag beside her. She was leaving. Miracle of miracles.

"Mom, what's going on?" Kelly asked, trying not to feel too excited that she was getting her house back.

"I'm leaving, Kelly."

"And going where? You don't have a home."

"She's coming to live with me," a voice said from the kitchen. She knew that voice like her own, and when Vivienne appeared in the doorway, her suspicions were confirmed.

"Vicki?"

"Vivienne," she and her mother corrected at the same time.

Kelly didn't acknowledge the correction and continued. "What are you doing here?"

"I came to get Mom. We're getting a place together in Atlanta."

"What?" Kelly said. Her sister was definitely up to no good. Why else would she leave Paris and her husband to come take care of their mother in Atlanta?

"I wanted to help, so I decided to come home, get mom and get her back on her feet again," she said, walking up behind their mother and rubbing her shoulder. Edie looked up and smiled adoringly. The whole thing made Kelly sick to her stomach.

"Okay, sis, what's the angle?" Kelly heard herself blurt out. But it was true. She knew there was an angle to be had somewhere, and Vivienne would always find it. If there was a loophole to be exploited, she'd uncover it and ride it until the wheels fell off.

"I resent that, Kelly. Why would I need an angle to come take care of my mother?"

"Well, you haven't been home in years, so…"

"I contacted her," Edie admitted.

"What? Why?"

Vivienne sat down next to her mother on the sofa and held her hand. Ick.

"Because I know you don't want me here, Kelly. We both know that. We're not the same kind of person, and that's okay. I know you love me in your own way, and I love you in my own way, but we can't live together."

Kelly knew what she was saying was true, but it still hurt to be basically abandoned and criticized by her own mother all over again. It wasn't anything new, but pain is pain.

"So you called the person who abandoned you?" Vivienne looked at her with a snarl.

"I didn't abandon our mother. I just made a better life for myself, and I think mother appreciates the courage that took for me."

"Oh please. Courage? You were a stripper and found a sugar daddy, simple as that!" Kelly shouted. It was the first time she'd ever stood up to her sister and spoke her mind.

"Kelly!" Edie yelled as she stood up.

A part of her wondered why she was fighting so hard about this because it was exactly what she wanted - for her mother to move and leave her in peace. Or was it?

Dang it, maybe she was just as dysfunctional as the rest of them. She didn't want her mother to live with her, but she wanted her mother to WANT to live with her?

"Vivi, can I talk to Kelly alone for a minute please?" Edie said. Vivienne walked outside to have a cigarette and the two women sat down.

"Mom, you know this is about the money, right?" Surely her mother had to know that Vivienne had her own intentions, and they weren't always honorable ones.

"Yes, I know full well what I'm doing, Kelly." For the first time in many years, Edie sounded sane and coherent.

"Then why are you doing it? As soon as the insurance money comes in, if it does at all, she's going to swindle you out of it."

136

"You know, all of my life has been spent wanting people to love me," Edie said. "First, your father, who was completely the wrong man for me, and then you kids. I so wanted to be the perfect mother and wife, but through poor choices or maybe fate or a little bit of karma... well, that just didn't happen." Kelly could see tears welling in Edie's eyes for a moment, but she willed them away. "For a long time, I wished so much for a relationship with you two girls, but I couldn't get over my own demons. I couldn't let anyone in."

"And that's why you became a hoarder..." Kelly said softly. It all made sense.

"Maybe. I don't know. I just wanted to be loved and accepted, but I don't do vulnerability well."

"Yeah, I can see that," Kelly said with a laugh. Edie smiled back at her.

"I know who Vivi is. She's a lot like me, so she can't really pull a fast one on me. Her husband dumped her for a younger woman, Kelly."

"Oh...."

"But don't tell her I told you that. She's pretty much destitute at this point. I've got some money put away, not a whole lot, but enough to get us through until the insurance gets settled. For once, I want to be the hero in someone's life. You don't need me, Kelly, but she does."

Being able to sit and talk to her mother like this seemed like a dream. It had never happened, and she liked it. And for a moment, she longed to get back all of those years with her mother that drugs took away. And now here she was, losing her again in a totally new way.

A part of her wanted to ask her mother to stay, to continue trying to mend their relationship. But she knew that it was impossible. Her mother was convinced that she didn't need her and that Vivienne did, which was probably true. Kelly had learned to be very resourceful and independent during her life, and she appreciated the fact that her mother apparently realized that.

"You know that if you ever need me, I'm just a phone call away. It hasn't been easy living here together, but I would like to think that we can spend more time together from now on." Kelly couldn't believe the words she was saying, but it was true. Her relationship with her mother would never be normal by other people's standards, but just being able to have a conversation – an honest one – was a step in the right direction.

"I know, and thank you. I would love to be able to spend more time together as a family. I know I wasted a lot of years, Kelly, with my problems. I let them get the best of me, no doubt. But, I would like to make that up to you girls in some way. Maybe we can even take a family vacation or something when my insurance money comes in!" The thought of going on an extended vacation with her mother made her want to run out into traffic, but she wasn't about to say that out loud.

They both stood up, facing each other. For a moment, Kelly surveyed her mother's face. Wrinkles had replaced her once smooth skin, and she had aged earlier than most people from living a hard life. The crows feet around her eyes were from too much laughing, and the lines around her mouth were from smoking cigarettes for too many years to count. But this was her mother, like it or not, and in that moment she was able to accept her for who she was.

So she did what all good daughters do – she reached out and gave her a hug. At first, her mother didn't return the embrace, but slowly she felt her arms slide up and around her. It felt strange, foreign, but Kelly remained there, willing herself to feel the feelings of a mother and daughter relationship even if just for a brief moment. Her once a year Mother's Day hugs had always felt uncomfortable, but this one became easier as the moments passed.

"I guess I better get going. Vivienne and I are staying at a hotel tonight, but we're moving into our new place tomorrow. I hope you'll come see it soon," her mother said as she pulled back from their embrace.

"I will. I promise," Kelly said. He crazily enough, she meant it.

CHAPTER 12

*M*eeting with the accountant for her business was one of the things that Kelly hated the most in the world. She definitely wasn't a numbers person, but she had worked really hard in her adult life to make sure that she understood her own finances. After watching two completely irresponsible parents during her formative years, it was amazing that she had any money at all in her checking and savings accounts.

But, she did. In fact, she had learned to squirrel away pretty substantial amounts of money in the last few years. Her business was doing well, and her dream was to buy her own building at some point. Although she did love renting where she was, she wanted to say that she owned something other than her house.

Still, meeting with an accountant was akin to

getting a root canal or a Pap smear – it was something she had to do but wasn't exactly looking forward to it.

Plus, if she was honest with herself, she didn't like the idea of not getting to see Quinn until later in the morning. They had become quite an item, even going out on a few more dates around town. She knew she was falling in love with him, but she definitely wasn't going to be the one to say it first.

They spent a lot of nights at his cabin, sitting on the dock and watching the sun set over the mountains. He was a fabulous cook. Who knew? He was constantly opening bottles of wine, grilling steak and he could make a mean cheesecake. The perfect man. Finally.

He texted her all throughout the day, which was funny given the fact that he was usually right upstairs. They were a lot alike, and very different. But she couldn't imagine living her life without him which was something she didn't expect after hating his guts when she first met him.

Still, because of her past, she had a really hard time trusting him completely. Everyone in her life had always let her down at some point, so it was very hard to trust that he wasn't going to just leave her. Sometimes she found herself wondering if he had a really dark past that she didn't know about, like maybe he was in member of the underground Whiskey Ridge mafia.

But he was definitely the most steadfast person she'd ever had in her life. She could predict what he was about to do at any given time. They finished each other sentences, he was never late for dates and he always called her when he said he would. All of the stability almost made her feel uncomfortable.

"Good morning," Cat said when Kelly finally got in to work. "How'd it go with the accountant?"

"Oh it was a wonderful time with lots of twists and turns and excitement," Kelly said dryly. Cat smiled and handed her some mail that had been piling up. "What are you doing here so early?" Kelly asked since Cat usually didn't come in until closer to her shift that started at six o'clock.

"Mrs. Stanley wanted to come in for a private yoga lesson this morning. She's got an upcoming 30th high school reunion, so she needs some extra help toning and tightening to impress those young men who didn't pay her any attention way back then," Cat said laughing. "And then Maggie had a dental appointment, so I told her I'd just watch the office. Our appointments are pretty light this morning anyway."

"Oh that's right. I forgot about Maggie's appointment."

"By the way, what was Quinn doing it your house so early this morning? It looked like he was about to do yard work or something. You must have him trained pretty good!" Kelly had no idea what she was talking about.

"Quinn wasn't at my house this morning. In fact, I left around seven o'clock."

"Um, he was most definitely there. I saw his truck pulled off at the side of the road and he was in the edge of your woods near that cross where the accident happened."

"He was? I have no idea what he would be doing there. In fact, he told me that he had a doctor's appointment this morning and wouldn't be in until around the same time I was. We're supposed to have lunch together."

"I almost didn't recognize him with a baseball cap on."

And there it was. The sentence that put everything together in her mind. The man that she had been seeing the last several months in front of her house was Quinn.

At first, she felt sorry for him all over again. But then it occurred to her that he had been keeping this secret for some reason. He hadn't told her that it was his wife who had died at the top of her property. But why?

As Cat walked out to grab an early lunch, Kelly sat at her desk staring at the flickering mouse in front of the search engine. She typed in "Penny Maverick" and waited.

Sure enough, she found the story from their local

newspaper from the day after Penny had died. And there it was in black and white print on the computer screen:

Penny Maverick passed away yesterday in a fiery car crash at the curve on Sycamore Road. She leaves behind her husband, Quinn, and her mother, Sally Ellington. Services will be held...

How had she never known this information? In an effort to put that terrible day out of her mind, she had forgotten the woman's first name. And Quinn certainly hadn't offered the information during their many times together.

Just as she closed her computer, Maggie came walking in from her dental appointment. She could tell that something was wrong with Kelly by the look on her face and immediately sat on the edge of her desk.

"What's wrong, boss? You look like you've seen a ghost."

"I have."

"What? You mean here?" Kelly had forgotten how ghost-phobic Maggie was. She claimed that she had grown up in a house where they had many ghosts who wouldn't move over to the other side, so anytime someone mentioned a ghost she got completely freaked out. She wouldn't even dress up on Halloween because of it.

"No. Sorry, I didn't mean an actual ghost. Can I talk to you about something?"

"Of course. As long as it isn't ghosts," Maggie said laughing. Kelly wasn't in a laughing mood.

"Do you remember me telling you about Quinn's late wife and how he's never told me how she passed away?"

"Yeah, I remember."

"Well, I just found something out and I don't what to do about it."

"You mean about his wife?"

"Yes. Cat was driving past my house this morning and she saw Quinn out at the cross marker for the terrible accident that happened there last year. It was his wife, Maggie," Kelly said, trying desperately to hold back tears.

"Oh my gosh. Why wouldn't he tell you that?"

"That's exactly what I'm wondering. Do you think it's possible he's been using me just to have access to the property? Or maybe like he feels close to his wife there or something?"

"I would have a really hard time believing that. He seems so into you. I mean, ya'll seem be so close. I can't see how he could possibly be pretending or trying to scam you."

"I don't know what's going on, but I intend to find out."

"Kelly, be careful. You don't want to jump to conclusions and ruin what could be a really good thing."

* * *

AS THE MINUTES PASSED, Kelly got more and more riled up in her office. She was supposed to be meeting Quinn for lunch, but she honestly didn't know if she wanted to go. What on earth was he thinking? Why would he keep something like that from her?

One part of her felt really bad for him, this man who had lost his wife in such a horrific way. The other part of her wondered what kind of game he was playing that he wouldn't share this secret with her. She felt completely conflicted and unsure of how to proceed.

After all, she didn't want to seem witchy like she didn't care that this poor guy has lost his wife. She also expected honesty from anyone she might choose to date, men especially, given recent circumstances with Rio.

"Hey. I thought we were meeting at the sandwich shop?" Quinn said, standing in the doorway of her office. Dang it. She was so caught up in her own thoughts that she had completely forgotten they were supposed to meet ten minutes before.

"Oh. I'm sorry. I got caught up in something here..." She was pretty sure he knew she was lying since looking around the office it was fairly obvious she was doing nothing. She was literally sitting in a chair, staring straight ahead and her computer was closed on her desk.

"Are you okay? You don't look well." He walked toward her and knelt in front of her with his hand on her knee. She suddenly felt extremely uncomfortable and stood up.

"I'm fine. Listen, maybe we can do lunch another day..." she said as she made her way around her desk and opened her computer.

"Kelly, come on. I know you, and something is definitely wrong. Are you mad at me?"

She looked up at him and found it very hard to be angry. Looking into those deep green eyes of his made her go completely weak, so she turned her attention back to the computer.

"No. Why would I be mad at you? It's not like you've been keeping something from me, right?" She looked up at him again, and a look of confusion clouded his face. She wanted him to admit it, right here and now, but it wasn't happening.

"Not that I know of..."

"Can I ask you something?"

"Of course."

"Have you been using me?"

"What? Using you? What would make you think that?" Now he looked more than confused.

"Cat saw you this morning at my house."

"Yeah... I went by... I thought you were going to be home..."

Kelly shot up out of her chair, angry that he was trying to cover his tracks even now. "Don't you do that, Quinn! Don't you lie to me! You at least owe me honesty. You knew full well I wasn't there, and I know exactly why you were there."

He looked defeated, obviously knowing that she knew the secret. He took a big breath in and slid down into the chair, hanging his head in his hands for a moment before looking up.

"I'm sorry. I should've told you."

"I don't understand. I thought… I thought things were moving along with us. I… I guess I just don't understand why you would keep something like this from me."

He shook his head. "Honestly, I don't know. I did want you to think that I was only interested in you for a connection to my late wife. And truly, I didn't want to tell you the real story of what happened to her and to our marriage."

She knew there had to be more, and this was obviously it. A part of her wanted to let him off the hook and not pry into this very personal part of his life, but the other part of her felt she was owed an explanation before they even tried to move forward in a relationship. And did she even want a relationship with him now? And did he want one with her?

"Quinn, you know I've had a long history of people not being honest with me. It takes a lot for me to open up, so if you have any plans to move forward with me then I have to know the truth. If not, it's okay for you to keep those things private and we can to stay friends, or least coworkers."

Every part of her wanted him to say that he would tell her everything, be totally open and transparent. But another part of her didn't know if she was worth it for him to give up all of his secrets just to be with her.

"I can't talk about this right now," he said, suddenly standing up and moving toward the door. "I know you don't understand, but I'm just not ready. I care about you, but I'm not ready to let anybody into that part of my world yet. I'm sorry."

And with that, he walked out of her office, out of the door and possibly out of her life.

* * *

KELLY SAT on her front porch, staring toward the cross at the road. She hadn't seen Quinn for the rest of the day. From what she could tell, he put one of the other instructors in charge and left. She hoped that he would come back soon, and maybe he just needed some time to think.

For her entire life, she'd never been important enough to anyone for them to be honest with her and take care of her. She worried that Quinn was just another in the long line of men who would disappoint her, but the pit of her gut told her that he was a different kind of man. That he was just struggling with something right now and he would come around. At least she hoped that was the case.

As she sat sipping her coffee, she thought about her life and where it was headed. Maybe she would be one of those women who always lived alone, with her cat and no husband. Maybe some women were just meant to live that life, and they probably enjoyed it. Yeah, that definitely wasn't her. She wanted more. She wanted the whole thing – the husband, the kids, maybe even the white picket fence.

She was a little surprised at just how quiet her home seemed all of the sudden. Just not having her mother's presence had left a bit of a void that she hadn't expected at all.

And just as she was lamenting the current state of her life, her cell phone dinged. It was her mother, and it looked like drama was about to unfold in her life all over again.

KELLY DROVE toward Atlanta like a bat out of hell. Her mother had texted her and said that Vivienne had emptied what little was in her bank account and disappeared a few hours earlier. And now Edie sat in her new apartment without a dime to her name.

When Kelly called her, she sounded frazzled,

anxious and full of anger. The anger was definitely legitimate.

She pulled into her mother's apartment complex and made her way up the stairs as fast as she could. If she could get her hands on her sister right now, she would ring her neck. But this was typical Vivienne – always an angle, no care about anyone else.

"Mom?" Kelly said as she knocked on the door and it opened on its own. She found her mother sitting on the sofa, drinking a beer and visibly shaking. "Mom, look at me."

"I can't believe she did it. I was trying to help her, be a mother to her. She stole everything I had. Every dime I have in my account is gone. She emptied it and then took off. How could she do that to me? She's my daughter."

"We need to call the police," Kelly said, fumbling to get her cell phone out of her purse. Her mother reached over and grabbed her hand.

"No. I'm not calling the police."

"You're kidding me, right? She's a thief. She needs to be reported and caught."

"She's my daughter."

"You can't be serious. You're going to let her get away with this? She took everything you have. She scammed you, plain and simple. She's probably doing this to other people too. We have to let somebody know," Kelly said again.

"I made her that way, Kelly. This is just karma

coming back to bite me in the butt." Edie took a long sip of her beer and leaned back on the sofa, letting out a sarcastic laugh. "I don't even know if she was ever married to the French guy. She was probably just over there scamming people."

"So, I guess you need to come home with me then?" Kelly said, a bit of hopefulness in her voice which was surprising even to her.

"Well, I can't stay here. Rent is due in three days and I don't have the money to pay it. I guess I'm going to have to get a job."

"I know of some openings in Whiskey Ridge," Kelly said with a smile. "In fact, I know that the coffee shop is hiring as well as the bookstore."

"You'd let me move back in with you?" Edie asked, the sound of surprise plainly evident in her voice.

"Of course I was, Mother. I told you, I want a second chance for us to really be mother and daughter but we have to have some ground rules."

"Ground rules? Here we go again… You and your tightly wound personality…"

"That's ground rule number one. You can't be criticizing me all the time. I'm a grown woman with my own way of doing things, so you're going to have to respect me and in return, I will respect you."

"Fine. Ground rule number two is that you'll stop dredging up the past at any opportunity. I know I screwed up. I've apologized, and I'd like to be able to move on without that always hanging over my head," her mother said.

"I can accept that. Ground rule number three is that you cannot start hoarding again. We will keep Gertrude on to do the basic cleaning once a week, but you're going to have to make an effort not to junk up your room. I don't want a repeat of what happened to your house."

"It's a deal."

With that, Kelly made some phone calls to her mother's landlord and helped her pack to head back to Whiskey Ridge. Life was never going to be the same. In fact, it was probably going to be chaotic and crazy and not the quiet serenity she'd been used to for so many years. And right now, that sounded incredibly perfect.

CHAPTER 13

As they drove through the dark Georgia night, thoughts flew through Kelly's mind. Everything had changed in the last few months. All of the ways she thought her life would be at this point were totally thrown to the wind.

She had a relationship that she really wanted, but now it might be gone. She had independence, but now her mother would be living with her long-term. The only stability she really had was her business, and now she wanted to hide from going there just to avoid an uncomfortable situation with Quinn.

Her life, in a word, was in upheaval.

"So where's your boyfriend?" her mother asked as they got closer to Whiskey Ridge.

"I don't have a boyfriend," Kelly said staring at the road in front of her.

"Okay, your male companion. Why didn't he

come with you tonight?"

"We're just fellow tenants in a building, Mom. Nothing else."

"I don't believe that. Spill it. What's going on?" her mother urged.

"I really don't want to talk about it tonight." She was tired, both mentally and emotionally, and she was still reeling from thoughts of strangling her sister, so having a long drawn-out discussion about Quinn wasn't something she wanted to do. Yet, she knew she was about to do it. Her mother was a bulldog that way.

"You know, I've been on this earth for quite some time. I might just have a little bit of advice to offer if you would actually tell me what's going on."

"Fine. As you know, his wife died over a year ago. I found out that he had been keeping something from me. The cross erected at the top of my driveway? That was his wife. She's the one who died in a car accident in front of my house and he never told me."

"So?" her mother said that she reached into her handbag for some lip gloss.

"So? So he lied to me. He was spending all kinds of time with me and even taking me out on dates, but he never told me. Don't you think that's pretty important?"

"Well, what I think is that you are being awfully self-centered in this situation, my dear."

"Thanks a lot! My girlfriends all agree with me. He shouldn't have kept that a secret."

"Then they're all wrong." Edie had a way of cutting right to the chase.

"Oh really? And why do you say that?" Kelly really was interested in hearing what her mother had to say. Her viewpoint on things was always unique, if not entertaining.

"Let me ask you this – when should he have told you?"

"I don't know… Maybe during our first date or after our first kiss or before our first kiss… I'm not sure, but he should've told me."

"And what makes you think he wasn't going to tell you soon?"

"I have no idea when or if he was ever going to tell me."

"Kelly, you've never been married. You've never had a relationship that was so complicated, except for maybe your relationship with me. So, when you first meet people, do you immediately launch into your entire history and talk about all of those things that embarrass you about your upbringing?"

"Of course not. I'm not telling that stuff to anybody that isn't going to remain in my life for a long time. It's hard for me to trust people and…" Suddenly, she got the point. Maybe he just didn't trust her enough or know her quite well enough to admit what had happened on the day his wife died and where she died. Maybe he had needed more time and instead of giving that to him, she had pushed and criticized.

"I think you see where I'm going with this. If you care about him, and I know that you do, then maybe you have to just give him some time to explain. Maybe you just have to leave some space open for people not to be perfect."

She couldn't believe that what her mother had just said was life-changing. It was true. She didn't leave space for people to be imperfect. She expected everyone to fall in line with her vision of what life was supposed to be like. And now, she had to make things right with Quinn whatever that meant.

BY THE TIME she had gotten her mother settled, it was after midnight and Kelly was exhausted. But she needed to make things right. And she couldn't wait a moment longer, so she jumped in her car and headed towards Quinn's house.

As she drove up the long driveway, she worried that he might come outside and shoot her thinking someone was breaking in, so she sent him a quick text message and asked him to come outside. He probably thought she was a lunatic showing up at his house after midnight, but she knew she'd never be able to sleep until she hashed things out with them.

He walked outside, wearing only a pair of plaid pajama bottoms and no shirt. It was almost more than her eyes could take.

"Hi," she said as she walked toward him. "Before you say anything, I know that it's crazy for me to be here so late at night and I hope I didn't wake you up."

"I couldn't sleep," he said.

"Me either. In fact, I just got back from bringing my mother home from Atlanta... again."

"What? What happened?"

"Long story, but let's just say that my sister ran off with everything my mother had including all of her money in her bank account."

"Oh no... So she's living with you again?"

"Yes, but I'm okay with it. We set some ground rules, and I feel really good about it. I think it's going to be nice to have a second chance."

"Second chances are good. I'm happy for you." There was such a sadness in his voice, and she wasn't sure if it was because of his wife or what had happened to their brand-new, budding relationship.

"I came here tonight to apologize for pushing you. I was only thinking about myself, and I should've realized that maybe you're dealing with your own stuff. I've never lost anyone who's close to me and I have no idea what you're going through. I just wanted you to know that."

"Kelly, I want you to know I wasn't keeping anything from you because I was using you in some way. In fact, I tried not to come to your house a lot because it brought about a terrible reminder for me. I came to your house because I wanted to see you despite the pain it caused me to pass that memorial. But, I just needed some more time to deal with it. I need to be honest with you about the story leading up to her crash."

"Quinn, you don't have to tell me anything right now. You don't owe me anything."

He walked toward her and put his hands on her upper arms. "I do owe you something. I never expected to feel this way about another woman, and certainly not the woman who lives on the property where my wife died. This has all been really confusing for me, but I know that I want to move forward... with you. That is if you're still interested?"

She looked up at him, rose up on her tippy toes and kissed him on the cheek. "I absolutely want to move forward with you. And I want to be here for you no matter what, so you can trust me. No pressure."

"Come inside," he said, sliding his arm around her and walking her to the front door. The house was dark except for one lamp on in the living room. She sat down on the sofa, and he sat across from her on the coffee table. She could tell that he was gearing up to give her the full story, and he was full of anxiety already.

"You don't have to do this tonight. Sleep. We can talk about this later..." she said, trying to give him an out but he shook his head.

"I need to do this now." She nodded her head in agreement and held both of his hands. "I told you that Penny and I were having marital issues for a long time. We talked about divorce, and then we'd get back together. I just hated the thought of giving up on a marriage. The day before she died, I asked for a divorce. I found out that she was cheating on me, and that was just the last straw."

"So why was she in Whiskey Ridge?"

"Her uncle is an attorney, and he lives about ten minutes from here. That morning, she had come by my karate studio and we argued about money and property and the fact that she cheated on me. So when she left me, she was pretty upset. Then she called me when she got into Whiskey Ridge and admitted she was pregnant with the guy's kid. I knew it wasn't mine because we weren't... well, you know... for a long time because things were so bad. She said she had broken it off with the guy she was cheating with and would be devoted to me, but I couldn't do it. I just couldn't raise this guy's child. The trust was gone, and I said no. For the first time in our relationship, I said no. She was really upset and hung up on me. The next call I got was from the local police department..."

A stray tear rolled down his cheek as he told the

story, and Kelly reached up and wiped it away. She stood up and then sat on his lap and hugged him. He buried his face in her shoulder, and she could feel the wetness of his tears through her shirt. This man, this rugged and handsome man, had been beating himself up with guilt for over a year now.

"Quinn," she said, her mouth pressed against his ear, "it wasn't your fault."

"I know that now," he said, sitting up and looking at her. "But it took me a long time to believe that. And when I realized that you lived on the spot where she died, it was a lot to take in."

"It must've been so hard for you, that night that you brought me home with my mother. I can't imagine what you must've thought when you realized where I lived."

"It was a shock, for sure. But there was a part of me wondering if it was also a sign that sometimes an ending can also be the beginning."

She wasn't sure that she had ever heard something more beautiful come from anyone's lips. Sometimes, endings were beginnings. The ending of her relationship with Rio. The ending of her relationship with her sister. Each of those occurrences had led to new beginnings. She had a new beginning with her mother and now she had a new beginning with Quinn, at least she hoped so.

"I have to ask you something," she said.

"Okay."

"Is it going to be too hard to be with me knowing where I live?"

"No. Not anymore. I grieved the loss of the relationship I once had with my wife a long time ago. And sometimes I go to the marker to honor that in some way, I guess. And maybe I felt guilty, but I don't anymore. I can't bring her back, and I can't change what happened, but I can start over. I can learn to trust again and open myself up to new possibilities." He pushed a stray hair out of her eyes.

"And could one of those new possibilities be with me?" Kelly asked with a smile. When his lips met hers, she had her answer.

"I love you, Kelly Cole, you stiletto-wearing-tightly-wound chick," he said with a smile. "But you still have to keep those heels off my floor."

"And I love you, Quinn Maverick, you loud-mouthed-knight-in-shining-armor terrible fisherman," she said giggling.

With that, he swept her up into his arms and straight down the hall into his bedroom where he would spend time showing her exactly all of the things he was good at even if fishing wasn't one of them.

* * *

SEE a list of all of Rachel's books at www.RachelHannaAuthor.com.

Made in United States
Orlando, FL
14 April 2024

45794527R00104